# EVENING

# SUSAN MINOT

# EVENING

Alfred A. Knopf

New York

1998

*For John Wang with best regards and admiration for Maine*

*[signature]*

THIS IS A BORZOI BOOK
PUBLISHED BY ALFRED A. KNOPF, INC.

Copyright © 1998 by Susan Minot

www.randomhouse.com

Library of Congress Cataloging-in-Publication Data
Minot, Susan.
Evening / Susan Minot. — 1st American ed.
p.      cm.
ISBN 0-375-40037-0 (alk. paper)
I.  Title.
PS3563.I4755E84      1998
813'.54—dc21                          98-15437
                                    CIP

Manufactured in the United States of America
Published October 12, 1998
Reprinted Twice
Fourth Printing, November 1998

*In Memory of*

SAM LAWRENCE (1929–1994)

SCOTT SOMMER (1950–1993)

ALEXIS ULLMANN (1958–1992)

*I give it to you not that you may remember time, but that you might forget it now and then for a moment and not spend all your breath trying to conquer it.*

WILLIAM FAULKNER

# CONTENTS

# ONE

# 1. THE CANOPY

*A new lens passed over everything she saw, the shadows moved on the wall like skeletons handing things to each other. Her body was flung back over a thousand beds in a thousand other rooms. She was undergoing a revolution, she felt split open. In her mattress there beat the feather of a wild bird.*

Where were you all this time? she said. Where have you been?

I guess far away.

Yes you were. Too far away.

They sat in silence.

You know you frightened me a little, she said. At the beginning.

No.

You did.

He smiled at that.

You looked as if you didn't need anyone, she said.

But those are the ones who need the most, he said. Don't you know that?

I do now, she said. Too late.

Never too late to know something, he said.

Maybe not, she said. But too late to do any good.

*   *   *

She lifted the yellow suitcase and banged it against her leg. She dragged it over the polished floor. The ceiling of Grand Central towered above her with arches and glass panes and squares of sunlight.

She was not late and did not have to hurry. The clerk in the window bowed his forehead like a priest in confession and pushed her ticket through. Across the great domed room she spotted a redcap with a cart and though she usually would have carried her bag to save money decided this was a special occasion. She was on her way to a wedding. She signaled to him.

The redcap flung her suitcase onto his cart. Whoever you're going to meet, he said, he's a lucky guy.

The heat in New York had been terrible and the air underground at the gate was heavy and close. When the train came out of the tunnel she saw thunderheads turning the sky yellow and grey. The rain started, ticking the window with scratches then pouring over it in streams. Crowds of cat-tails surged in a wave as the train blew past. By the time they reached Providence the rain had stopped and it was hot again with a hot wind blowing in the open doors. The engine shut off and they waited in the station. No new passengers got on. It was as if the world had paused on this late morning in July. She held her book loosely and watched out the window.

The station in Boston was shadowed in scaffolding dark as a cave with bands of light on the paneled benches and few travelers. The redcap who took her bag was young and did not say a word. He pushed a contraption with a bad wheel and had trouble steering through the door. She came out of the damp entranceway into the brightness of the turn-around beyond where she saw among the parked cars the dark green woody. The doors were open and she saw in front Buddy Wittenborn and in the driver's seat Ralph Eastman and a third person with his back to her. The person was standing with one foot up on the running board. When she got close Ralph caught sight of her and jumped out of the car and Buddy looked over with a lazy smile. Only when she was near did the back turn around and the long leg come off the running board and she saw the man's face. He was wearing squarish dark glasses so she couldn't see his eyes. She noticed his mouth was full though set in a particular firm way, the combination of which affected her curiously. She felt as if she'd been struck on the forehead with a brick.

The person's face seemed lit from within.

Ralph Eastman gave her a kiss on the cheek asking how was the career girl from New York and Buddy Wittenborn slid off the front seat and hugged her and ducked back turning his head and pushing his glasses back on his nose. He was wearing a disheveled shirt buttoned up wrong and a belt outside the belt loops and even with the beanie on his head looked as always handsome.

Ralph tipped the redcap, taking charge of the bags. She was trying to look at any other place other than at the person in the sunglasses.

Oh, Buddy said. This is Arden.

She was far enough away from the person that not to shake his hand was not rude. She didn't dare shake his hand. Hi, she said and smiled brightly. Her handbag fell to the ground.

That's Ann, Buddy said.

Hello Ann. The person had a deep voice which came from somewhere deep in his chest. We've been waiting for you, Ann. It was also kind of rough.

She caught a lipstick rolling and looked up. The person was not smiling. She blushed and looked back down. Am I that late? We stopped for a while in Providence . . . She felt the black glasses facing her.

Ralph slammed the back hatch. A late train has been figured into the calculations.

He's sure we'll miss the ferry, Buddy said.

On the contrary, just what I plan to avoid. So let's go.

The person was walking away from the car. He bent to pick something off the ground.

Harris, Ralph called, starting the car.

The person came back on long slow legs and got into the back-seat beside Ann. It was an old woody and the windows tilted in. He held up some keys attached to a Saint Christopher medal. These yours? he said.

God, Ann said, taking her keys. Thank you. That was idiotic. She looked straight at him. Which is your name?

They both are.

In what order?

Which is better? The face was placid and she could not read the eyes behind the glasses.

I don't know. They're both good.

No, the person said and he smiled for the first time. One is always better.

It was 1954 and Ann Grant was twenty-five years old.

They drove north. She liked being the girl in a car with three boys. They drove through Revere where the water was purple at the shore and the highway was raised above the tract houses, past gas stations with enormous signs shaped like horses, and miniature golf courses with waterfalls and orange dinosaurs. They passed motels with teepee cabins and restaurants shaped like pagodas and restaurants shaped like barns with plastic cows outside. They exited to Danvers winding past steeples and fudge stores with pink script writing back onto the highway where green countryside flickered out the window behind the person's profile. His name was Harris, Ralph was the one to say, Harris Arden. She sat beside Harris Arden in the backseat and they talked and now and then he turned toward her. He'd grown up in Virginia, was born in Turkey, had lived in Switzerland. His father was a diplomat, raised in St. Louis, his mother was Turkish which explained his coloring. Harris Arden lived in Chicago now, he said, and worked in a hospital.

Then Ann Grant realized who he was. He was Doctor R, Carl's friend, whom he'd served with in Korea. But it wasn't Doctor R as she had thought but Doctor Ar for Arden. She had pictured some-one older.

You're the musician, she said.

Not so much anymore.

Isn't your band playing at the wedding?

What's left of it.

And you're a doctor too? Buddy said, prying open a beer with a Swiss Army knife. Who wants a cold one?

No one took him up on it. The person didn't seem to hear and stared out the window.

Ann sings, Ralph said, facing forward driving.

Does she? The person looked interested.

Just for fun, Ann said. Just in little places.

In New York little places are pretty big.

These really are little, she said. It's not even my job.

Ann's a pretty good singer, Buddy said.

I'd like to hear her sing, said the person in the sunglasses looking ahead.


Have you moved her?

She was sitting up this morning. Mrs. Lord.

The smell of rose water.

I'm sorry I'm late, said Ann Lord. We stopped for a long time in Providence.

Mrs. Lord, you have a visitor.

Ann Lord opened her eyes. No he's not, she said. It wasn't a visitor, it was Dr. Baker.

Afternoon Ann. Mercifully Dick Baker did not shout at her. His sleeves were rolled above the elbows, a stethoscope hung around his neck.

Afternoon, she said. I look a fright.

Nonsense, he said. You've never looked a fright. He came in every other day. Dick Baker was a friend of the Lords' and used to come often to dinner parties when Oscar was still alive—they had entertained more then—and as he held Ann Lord's wrist he remembered once watching her leave the dining room and disappear down the dark hallway toward the kitchen. She'd been wearing a dress with a pink sheen to it and the sheen had retained the light after her legs and arms and head had disappeared in the gloom. He checked her pulse against his watch, remembering the sheen.

After a while she said, Where am I?

You're in Cambridge in the house on Emerson Street. His dry fingers pressed near her ears. He wasn't looking at her, feeling around the way doctors do, as if they're blind.

I don't mean that, she said, fixing him in her gaze. That's not what I mean.

You're doing fine.

Dick.

He had bent over the beds of many patients, but it was always different when you knew the person. It had an extra dimension to it. Dr. Baker was not a spiritual man. He considered himself a practical man. His job was simply to figure out what the heck the problem was and do his damndest to fix it and if he couldn't then move on and hope with the next one he could. He had been as straightforward with her as he was able. The treatment might give her some time but as far as curing this type of cancer . . . no that wasn't likely. There was no doubt about it when you knew the person the job changed. He felt less effectual when he knew more of the person's life. Not that he knew a great deal about Ann Lord. She was one of those mysterious women, not that he knew a great deal about women either. He knew she'd been married three times—the children came from the different husbands—and there was a hint of a racy life singing in nightclubs in New York which Dick Baker had never heard her mention and then that tragedy with her son . . . His wife Bertie said Ann Lord was just like other women, maybe a little more stylish if you had to say something, but like other women. Bertie frankly found her a little distant and cold. Dr. Baker found them all mysterious to a point and Ann Lord had her own brand of mystery. She always looked well turned out and was a little cool then she would surprise you with a little jolt of something witty and inviting. It was nearly flirtation and chal-

lenged something in him. Of course he did not relate that to his
wife. He knew that much about women.

How long Dick, she said.

It was not the first time she'd asked. They didn't always want to
know. More often than not they didn't want to know the truth.

Dick. Her hand took his sleeve.

Dr. Baker glanced back at the nurse who gave a sort of nod and
cast her glance to the side. He leaned down.

Let's just say you won't see the leaves change this year, he said.


When's Nina coming?

She can't come till Friday. She's in rehearsal.

I'd think she'd want to be here, said Aunt Grace. Constance has
come all the way from Paris. I'd think Nina could make it from
New York.

Mother understands, Margie said.

I hope she's right.

I think so, Constance said. Fergus, down.

Fergus, stop bothering Constance. She thinks she's a person,
Aunt Grace explained, gazing fondly at her terrier. I just hope Nina
doesn't regret it later.

It's Nina's big break supposedly, Margie said.

There'll be another break, said Aunt Grace. If she's good. Something else will come along. Your mother won't. Aunt Grace was an
unlikely ally of Ann Lord's. Her younger brother had been Ann's
second husband and when Ted Stackpole left her a widow Grace
had stepped in to help. Having no family of her own she had the
space to do it. She had never married and lived alone with her dog.

She'll be here this weekend, Margie said.

Let's hope Ann is lucid.

What do you mean? She's been lucid.

So far, said Aunt Grace mysteriously.

When Teddy came downstairs he looked as if he'd been away on
a long trip.

He's been up there an awful lot, Aunt Grace said. I hope he can handle it.

He's doing fine, Constance said.

So different from his father, said Aunt Grace. Teddy was Ted Stackpole's son. His father couldn't stand sick people.

She lay on her back staring up at the canopy. Her thoughts went round and round and it was like spinning staring up at the trees the way she used to when she was young. She could not focus or stop or hold onto a thought for very long. She watched things blur by and now and then a bright light like the sun flashed through the leaves. She saw the water lying in lozenge shapes in the marshes past Portland and a face like a mask with dark glasses on it. He was asking her where she worked. Where . . . she could not remember. It was either the bookstore or the auction house or doing errands for Mrs. Havemeyer or cataloguing for Mr. Stein. She remembered the plaid shirt Buddy Wittenborn had been wearing and the rattle of the woody with the windows open and how the summer light threw a fuzzed screen over the trees. She saw a tilted field of purple lupin, a sign which said Free Beets Monday but she could not remember which job she'd been at the day before, the jobs were all folded together, or which little apartment she'd been in, they were folded together too, the one on Sixty-eighth Street with the bay window and geranium, the one with the slanted floor above Madison, there was a punch-out clock in the basement of Scribners', a navy wool jacket she wore, the slippery rugs in Mrs. Havemeyer's foyer, smoke hanging in the air at Sling's, Fiona fishing an onion out of a martini glass, the streets Sunday morning Fifth Avenue deserted . . . it all floated by, random and nearly transparent. They were the props of her life but she had no more sense of them than one does for the stage scenery of a play one saw ages ago then forgot. No doubt at the time they affected her, stirred some reaction, irritated or pleased her, but now most of them gave off neither heat nor cold and she watched them drop into the gaping dark hole of

meaningless things she had not forgotten, things one level up from
the far vaster place where lay all the unremembered things.

Now vivid before her was the sight of a road narrowing up a hill
with humps of trees on either side like a gate and the frame of a
windshield thrumming and the back of Ralph Eastman's tidy haircut being blown in fingerprint gusts and Buddy swigging from his
beer, lips sideways. The car was moving forward but encased in
memory it seemed still and suspended, as if the configuration in
the car, the person beside her with his elbow resting on the window, his hand dangling, the skin darker at the knuckles, the window framing a sky of indistinct clouds and tall grasses flashing
by, as if it were a delicately rendered structure wired and bolted
together reflecting mirror-like the configuration of her heart.

She opened her eyes not knowing where she was. The room had
gotten dark. The pain rose in her and she remembered. That's
right, this is what she was now. In her sixty-five years Ann Lord had
kept herself busy and was not particularly reflective but now forced
to lie here day after day she found herself visited by certain reflections. Life would not hold any more surprises for her, she thought,
all that was left was for her to get through this last thing. But her
eyes were as sharp as ever and she saw everything that went by.

She knew the room. It had been her room for some time. She
had known other rooms and lived in other houses and been in
other countries but this was the last room and she knew what
was coming to her in it. It was coming to her slowly and the room
remained indifferent. The bedposts rose up with notched pine-
cones at the end and the narrow desk stood there shut with the
key in the keyhole and on the bureau were the silver frames with
her children in little squares and little ovals. The windows faced
two ways, toward the beech tree and the high fence with spear tips
separating it from the next yard and the near corner facing down to
the end of the garden and lawn and all the time she felt the engine
chugging quietly beneath her manufacturing pain ceaselessly. It
was not going fast enough. She wanted it to speed up but whenever
she urged it forward the effort only bound her faster to life. So she

pretended she wasn't trying, pretended she was being borne along at whatever speed the wheels wanted to take her, pretended indifference. She ought to be good at pretending, she thought, she'd had a lifetime of doing it.

Then she saw in the murky light the tombstone shape of a large bird sitting on the windowsill. It looked like an owl or a hawk. When it lifted to fly away it spread its wings and flapped once and glided out on stiff wings which seemed held up by string. Its round heavy body soared upward and she watched it with a beating heart till the canopy above her intervened and the bird was blocked from her sight.

So she had them remove the canopy. Constance and Margie rolled off the white ruffled cover while she sat tilted but erect in the armchair by the window in her Dior nightgown. Constance had done her hair like Empress Josephine with gold string and Margie looked like a gypsy with her long skirt and tangled hair. They clapped the wooden slats together like Chinese instruments and yanked up the bowed pieces bridging the posts. When she resumed her position in bed the room had opened up and she could see more. There were not so many things open to her now and she was not going to miss the few which were. She could see the upper windows and the upper walls and the whole of the ceiling.

She felt herself being drawn up. She left behind the making of plans and the wondering about the future and a strange anticipation visited her. Something was calling to her. She heard soft paws crossing the floor above her. A blur passed by the window, a cloud of fidgeting butterflies. She smelled sea water, she smelled burnt sugar. Someone was making a cake. The sound of fingernails scraped the wainscoting behind the bamboo bookshelf. She scanned the shelves of her life. First she was Ann Grant then Phil Katz's wife then Mrs. Ted Stackpole then Ann Lord. Bits of things swam up to her, but what made them come? Why for instance did she remember the terrace at Versailles where she'd visited only once, or a pair of green and white checkered gloves, a photograph of city trees in the rain? It only demonstrated to her all she would forget. And if she did not remember these things who would? After she was gone there would be no one who knew the whole of her life. She did not even know the whole of it! Perhaps she should have written some of it down . . . but really what would have been the point in that? Everything passed, she would too. This perspective offered her an unexpected clarity she nearly enjoyed, but even with this new clarity the world offered no more explanation for itself than it ever had.

They drove past houses set up on swollen banks, houses with four windows in front and four on the side with dark shutters against the clapboard, houses with porches, sometimes with American flags. They talked about music and found themselves in agreement on a number of small points of taste which Ann Grant found surprising but which the person did not seem to.

In Waldoboro they stopped for lunch at Moody's Diner which had green booths and Formica tables edged in aluminum. Ralph refused the clam roll fearing poison. Buddy had the meatloaf special and a hotdog and piece of pie. Harris Arden she remembered ordered a hamburger and black coffee. When his plate arrived the sunglasses came off.

He put them on the table. Ann looked instinctively away as one was taught to if there was an eclipse of the sun. Then she looked back. His eyes were very light which was a surprise with the caramel cast of skin, between light grey and blue. They squinted as if the world were too bright. He bit into his hamburger and chewed and the eyes looked for an instant at her then out the window. It was as if someone had pierced her chest. She felt it in her toes. It was a marvelous feeling. She picked up her grilled cheese with no appetite whatsoever.

Sitting in the diner among the dark shadows and gleaming curves with the bright day outside Ann Grant felt as if she were both a stranger to herself and more herself than she'd ever been. Her elbow lay on the table, the door swung open to the kitchen, the pine shadows darkened the back window, all was dense with meaning. For no reason that she could name she was overcome with a sense of destiny. Her body carried the conviction more than her mind, the sensation came over her slowly that something important was happening, there was a decidedly new quality to everything around her, things were sharper and brighter, the air amplified sound. She had not yet pinpointed the change to her having met this person, she was being too pleasantly carried along to need to name it. But something made her feel as if she were floating and it had begun the moment she'd seen the person's face.

❖  ❖  ❖

You forgot, she said.

I never forgot.

No?

I didn't.

Well, she said.

Don't be like that.

How would I know you never forgot?

You should have known.

How? How was I ever to know?

Ann, he said and took her hand.

Forgetting, remembering . . . why should I care?

I couldn't forget you, he said.

What difference does it make anyway? she said.

It makes a difference.

I don't know.

You made a difference, he said. You changed my life.

And I never got to see it, she said.

No.

Your life. I never got to see your life.

Nothing's perfect, he said.

No, she said.

They were both smiling.

# TWO

# 2. THE BALSAM PILLOW

The world shifted as if a piece of paper had been flipped and she was now living on its other side. Things turned transparent, the man one married, the house one lived in, the bracelet one wore, they all became equal to each other, equal motes of dust drifting by. Strange things were happening *something has already happened.* For two days a leaf the size of a ham hung in the air one foot from her face. She grew sensitive to the different shades of white on the ceiling. Her sense was not always right. The position of her arm had something to do with inviting people to dinner. She needed to move the pillow so a boat could dock there. She knew it wasn't logical and wondered if the drugs were obscuring things then it seemed as if the drugs were making it easier to read the true meaning.

*Let's turn ourselves a bit let's try a little lunch let's have a little sip let's sit a little up*

I'm not hungry.

Keep up our strength, said the nurse.

A wave of nausea swept through her. This is not what she'd planned, she'd always planned to go quickly. A man's shoulder was coming through the wall.

He's come back, said Ann Lord.

Who?

I thought he'd forgotten.

They always come back, said the nurse.

Ann Lord had never been sick before and yet it seemed now that this was the only day she'd ever had. She'd never had any other kind of day. It was a peculiar life she led. She lay here, she slept, people came in and stood and sat in chairs. Sometimes when she woke there were new people there and sometimes no one. Her children came in carrying flowers, carrying cups, carrying babies. A needle poked her. But she couldn't be that tiny white dot she saw in people's glasses, that wasn't herself. She had lived in different places, sailed boats by different islands, rode in many cars in many cities, and now as she lay staring up at the light and shadows moving above her found many things returning to her which she had forgotten. Her memory was turned inside out. It was in this frame of mind that Ann Lord chanced upon a small thing which had a most extraordinary effect on her.

It had been raining and the washed air came through the windows. Ann Lord woke to no shadows and grey air hanging over everything like the grey chiffon her mother used to leave draped over the chairs after a customer's fitting. The door to Oscar's room was open to the rustlings of the nurse.

Margie came in, a blur in an Indian dress, holding up something near her face. Smell this, she said. I found it upstairs in the chest.

Didn't they have better things to do than dig up old things in the attic?

She held it out. Ann Lord turned her cheek and felt the soft burlap. It was one of those little pillows filled with balsam needles sold in gift shops in Maine. *I pine for you and balsam too.* This one had no writing and the black stencil of the pinecone was partly rubbed off. She'd kept this thing for a reason and in a moment would remember. Yes. It was from Lila, from her wedding, a sort of joke present to her bridesmaids along with the silver perfume flask which Ann Lord still had right there on the glass shelf in the bathroom. She smelled the cushion and smelled the balsam and what happened to her then was a kind of wild tumult. The air seemed to fracture into screens which all fell crashing in on one another in a sort of timed ballet with spears of light shooting through and something erupted in her chest with a gush and in her mind's eye she saw her hands forty years younger and heard the clink of rocks on a beach and the sound of a motorboat and rising behind that came a black night and a band playing in the trees and the smell of water in the pipes of a summer cottage and she raised her hand to keep the cushion there and breathed in and heard an old suitcase snap open.

You O.K.? Margie said. Her face must have been strange.

It reminds me . . . she began, but couldn't say.

A dark cave was lit up and as she looked around at the shadowed inlets flickering in the torchlight she saw things and heard sounds she'd known long ago *stay like that always* the balsam smell made the torches flare up—a window full of fog footsteps on a grey porch stakes being hammered in the night. Something was dawning on her slowly, she kept the cushion on her bed, something was opening beneath her. It seemed to be her soul.

Something stole into her as she walked in the dark, a dream she'd had long ago. The air was so black she was unable to see her arms, it was a warm summer night. Above her she could make out the dark line of the tops of spruce trees and a sky lit with stars. She felt the warm tar through the soles of her shoes. The boy beside her took her hand.

Margie Katz and Constance Katz sat in chairs pulled over to the open back door of the kitchen.

Mother never really liked Seth that much to begin with, Margie said. So she thinks I'm better off now.

I never knew it had gotten that bad, Constance said.

It was pretty bad.

I never knew that.

Margie nodded. That was the whole thing really.

Luc drinks, Constance said. But only a lot in spurts. Everyone drinks in France. It's what they do, drink wine.

Margie looked into the darkness of the garden. Well I couldn't take it.

You shouldn't.

No.

So you're lucky you didn't have children, Constance said.

I guess.

Believe me, you are.

What, would you rather not have Julian?

Course not. I'm just saying it's not always easy if you're divorced.

I thought Will was being a good father.

He is, Constance said. He is, she added wearily. But the whole situation is confusing for Julian. He's got an English father who's remarried to an Italian and an American mother who works too much and everyone else around him is French.

That's what happens when you live in France, Margie said.

Well it's not that easy, the poor kid. Constance thought for a moment. And the man his mother lives with is half-Russian . . . or sort of lives with—I don't know what's going on with Luc. I don't think I understand French men.

Maybe Paris is the wrong place for you then.

I love Paris. Anyway I have to stay because Will's there and Julian has to see his father.

Children adjust to a lot, Margie said. Julian's a good kid.

I know he is. He's an angel. God knows how he got that way with me for a mother.

You want some more? Margie stood up and the tiny mirrors on her skirt flickered and the bracelet around her ankle jingled. She opened the freezer door. I'm just going to have a tiny bit more.

No thanks.

You sure?

Constance gazed past her crossed feet in their slender sandals. A bowl of melting ice cream with the spoon sticking up rested in the lap of her trimly cut linen pants. When did she redo this floor? Constance said.

This floor hasn't been redone.

It hasn't?

No.

Really?

It's the same floor it's always been, Con.

It is?

Yes. The little squares in the corner. It's always been this floor. I promise.

I swear I've never seen it before.

You have too.

Really.

You've been away too long, Margie said, sitting back down.

Constance stared at the floor. That is very weird, she said.

Margie ate some ice cream. Those earrings from Paris? she said.

Constance touched her ears. She had short curly hair and the earlobes peeked out. These, I got these in Rome.

They're nice. Just a little gold . . .

I think they're from Morocco originally.

Really nice.

The sisters sat in silence for a while.

So where is he now? Constance said.

Who?

Your ex-husband.

St. Kitts still.

Really. God.

That's where the boat is.

That's right. I forgot.

We're not really officially divorced yet, Margie said. Constance remained silent. He's still taking charters out.

My idea of a nightmare, Constance said.

It wasn't so bad. It was bad when you had a bad client. That was bad. But sometimes it was sort of great.

The phone rang.

I bet it's Teddy, Constance said.

Margie got up slowly and answered the phone. Yah, hi. She nodded at Constance. Fine. Yup, she's fine. I mean, you know, the same. Sleeping. No, me and Con. I took Nora to the Square. She *wanted* to take the subway. She's been here ten days without a break, she had to go home. I know, she's great. Another one, not the one who comes at night—what's her name? You know, the other one—

Gabby, Constance said.

What?

Gabby. That's her name. Gabby.

Margie looked annoyed and kept talking. She discussed the nurses' payment and when Teddy was coming the next day. After she hung up she said, One of the babies was screaming in the background the whole time.

The sisters burst into laughter.

We are bad, Margie said. This made them laugh harder.

Poor Teddy, Constance said and quieted down after a while, chuckling a little. God I am exhausted. Why? What have I done all day?

This is exhausting, Margie said. Let's face it.

I have to go to bed. Constance did not move.

What was that? Margie said.

What.

The door.

I didn't hear anything.

The brass knocker thumped at the front door.

Couldn't be, Constance said.

Who is that? said Margie.

Do we have to answer?

The lights are on.

The lights could be on.

The knocker thumped again.

It'll wake her, said Constance.

O.K. I'll get it. Margie stood up lazily. She pulled the tie out of her hair, rebunched it in a knot and wound it up with deft fingers. Her bare feet slapped gently down the hall.

She opened the door to a white-haired man in a light-colored suit standing on the porch. Behind him the shadows from the streetlight made a mottled pattern on the empty street and there was the occasional lit window hiding among the black leaves.

I'm looking for Ann Grant, the man said. His suit was wrinkled and a pale tie had a yellow egg-like stain on it. His halo of hair surrounded a large weathered face. He did not look like one of their mother's usual friends.

This is her house.

The man's head wobbled, then jerked still. You her daughter?

Yes.

The man looked her up and down. You must be Margaret then.

Margie started to smile, but something prevented her. Yup, she said.

Forgive me for disturbing you at this hour. It's terribly rude, I know. But you see I've just been at dinner—he glanced over his shoulder, then lurched forward—in Boston with my great old friends—the Beegins—and I've only just heard of your mother's— he pressed his chin into his chest—misfortune and wanted to pay my respects.

Margie folded her arms. The guy was hammered.

I'm only in town tonight and I was hoping I could . . .

It's pretty late. She's sleeping.

The man nodded solemnly.

Of course, he said, frowning. It's much too late. He began to sway a little. I do apologize for that. I don't know what came over me. I just thought . . . He looked at Margie and winced. He pursed his lips. I knew your mother a long time ago, he said. She was a wonderful singer. He bowed to the side. You can tell her—he put out a heel and swiveled his knee—oh, he said suddenly and held out a small brown paper bag which had been hidden in the shadows. The top was bunched together and tied with a shredded purple ribbon, already used. The name's John Winter.

The kitchen door flapped from deep behind her and Constance's footsteps then Constance herself came up to the doorway.

An old home remedy, he said. Forgive the presentation.

Margie took the bag. It was heavier than it looked. She put her other hand under it.

This is an old friend of Mother's, Margie said. John—Winter.

This is Constance.

Yes, I see that, he said and shook Constance's hand.

Nice to meet you, she said, leaning out and smiling. Would you like to come in? Too late she caught her sister's eye.

The man's gaze flicked toward Margie's face. Well, I . . . no, he said. I couldn't. Thank you anyway. I was telling your sister I have to be off early tomorrow and just wanted to pay my respects. But it has been lovely to meet Ann's daughters. I see her look in both of you. He was jerking his head, then freezing then swiveling, managing to keep his balance. Different, he said, but there in both of you.

Constance shot her sister a concerned look.

Oh, he said. Does she still sing?

What? said Constance.

I mean, not now, but did she keep on with her singing?

Not professionally, Constance said. But she always liked to sing.

Likes, Margie said. Still likes.

I can never hear "Summertime" without thinking of her, he said. Wonderful voice. He thrust his hand into his pocket. Well good night then.

Come back in the day, Constance said. I'm sure she'd like to see you.

He turned and stopped. His hand moved over his face. Around the mouth and jaw, he said, and he pointed at Constance.

We'll give her this, said Margie, holding up the bag.

The man took one step down then his shoulders heaved back as if he'd heard a sudden sound and he wheeled around to face them again. Quick story, he said. I once danced with your mother, it was at a wedding, all we did was go from one wedding to another in those days, and for some reason I found myself asking for romantic advice the way one does I suppose dancing with a beautiful woman. I had just gotten engaged, and was having misgivings about the girl. I don't know, maybe they were the natural fears. So your mother asked me if I trusted her. I said I did. She asked me if I would still like to see her when she was old and I said I thought I would. Then she asked me if we laughed together. And that stopped me. The man had become very still. Maybe he'd not been drunk after all. He now spoke clearly. Laughing was not something we did a lot of, the girl and I. But I thought about it some more and felt I loved her and did get married after all. He clapped his hands. After eighteen years we were divorced. I never forgot what your mother said. I don't know if that's a story or not. He looked at Margie then at Constance. Point is, I should have listened.

He raised his hand and again said good night and ambled down the path and onto the street. He hesitated. He did not seem to have a car.

Margie closed the door.

So what's in it? Constance said.

Should we look?

Of course we should look.

It feels strange, sort of soft, Margie said.

Constance untied the ribbon and they looked inside. They could see a dark red surface rounded and glistening within the folds of some flimsy butcher's paper.

What—that is disgusting, Constance said. I hope it's not human. What is it?

It looks like a liver, said Constance, and she shivered.

I think it's a heart, Margie said.

Throw it away.

Is it to eat? Margie mumbled.

Get rid of it, said Constance, walking off.

Do you think Mother really said that?

I don't know. It didn't really sound . . . Constance shrugged. Sure, who knows. Maybe.

Seth and I used to laugh a lot, Margie said.

She must have been different back then, Constance said.

Margie peered into the bag.

Throw it out, Constance said at the end of the hall. It's sick.

Really? Margie put her fist around the bag, closing the top. It doesn't seem that sick to me.


Where's my nurse? said Ann Grant Lord.

She's in the other room. Do you want me to get her?

Not that one. The other one, the Irish one.

She's off for two days, Margie said.

Where'd she go?

Home, Mother. She needed a day off.

Who's in there? Ann Lord's head did not move from the pillow but her eyes narrowed.

Another one filling in, Constance said. She leaned forward to whisper, I'm not sure her name.

What?

Another nurse, Constance said loudly.

I want the Irish one back.

Mother, you had a visitor last night, Margie said. Constance and Margie looked at each other.

Ann Lord looked at her hands on the bedspread.

His name was John Winter.

The head against the pillow remained still. The hands did not move. Never heard of him.

Really? John Winter? He said he danced with you at a wedding.

I don't know anyone by that name.

He knows you.

Yes, a lot of people say they do.

❄

The line between her dreams and waking life disappeared. She had no idea what day it was. They said it was July. A month had gone by since the last of the tests. A chilling phrase: run some tests. They made her drink poison, poked and prodded, pulled blood out in purple threads, then came Dick Baker's casual voice, Could she come into the office. She felt like hell, silence on the line. Why don't I stop by on my way home? he said, in this way telling her. Then the days at the hospital which is no place for sick people. There you blurred into something else in rooms with brown stripes down the halls and plastic under the sheets and curving aluminum bars and windows that didn't open. People wore crumpled masks and the furniture rolled. She lay under the machine shaped like a bull's head and needles were taped into place and needles pulled out. Visiting hours were over. In the middle of the night buzzers went off and in the morning when you rolled your I.V. by the next room saw the empty bed with the blank clipboard and no more bald woman named Gwenivere. She had brought her own nightgown not to wear the dreadful tie-things they gave you and always spilled her orange juice peeling off the top. No there was no question of her going back to the hospital.

There were days when it was true then it was not true then it was true again. After the treatment stopped she felt better then worse then she saw there was nothing to make it better. It quickly got worse. Dinner at the Welds' they were discussing war with dessert and Ann Lord got up from the table and found an armchair past the pocketdoors where she could still see them talking, she just couldn't listen anymore. It had come blasting up into her head and she couldn't hear anything. She tried to push at it with her will but it roared and roared. She was no match for it. Clare Weld came toward her holding a tilting coffee cup. Clare was not an affectionate woman, reserved with her husband and children, so it surprised Ann Lord when she put her coffee cup down, sat on the arm of Ann's chair and very naturally put a confident arm around her and kissed the top of Ann's head. Illness brought out surprising things in people.

She closed her eyes and saw sunlight in squares on the Turkish rug and didn't know if she was in a dream or not. Then she heard the wind and the sound of water and knew she was at the shore. The shore was never silent.

# 3. The Yellow Suitcase

She woke before dawn coughing. She could make out the shape of the glass of water on the table but it was too far to reach and after a while she managed to stop coughing without drinking.

She lay still as the room grew light. The blue ceiling turned grey then light grey. It was thoroughly quiet. It seemed to be the beginning of something more than just day. For a few long moments she lay and felt—what was it? The dawn light put her in mind of creation. It must have been this way on the actual first day of the world. A thin yellow light spread out and all the sorrows which sat in her seemed suddenly to lift up and fly off and were replaced with the most inappropriate hope. For what had she to hope for? A swift end perhaps. And yet her whole spirit was lifting, she felt hope not only for herself, but—it did sound absurd—for all humanity. She lay here on a trembling leaf and thought of all the other people lying on their leaves waiting for the sun to come up and it seemed that if they were quiet and patient what each of them wanted would eventually come. She was sure of it. An orange glow filled the room.

The glass on the bedside table began to sink. She closed her eyes for a moment to concentrate and the pain got worse. This was the darkness she would be looking at for a long time. She opened her eyes. The glass continued sinking. She could not see the water in it, only the top rim. She struggled to keep it in sight. The glass was going very slowly, but it was important that she see it the moment it disappeared. She smelled the pillow beside her.

A yellow suitcase came flying out of the fog, it was dragged over loose stones, thrown into a car, hauled over a polished floor. It lay open on a suitcase rack at the foot of a bed. She walked through stripes of light and shadow, something rattled, there had been rain in New Haven and a hot wind off the platform in Providence. They were waiting for her in Boston. Her lipstick rolled on the ground and the face with the sunglasses was luminous.


She sat in the backseat beside him with the windows down. Buddy drank more beer and fell asleep and Ralph refused any offers to drive because if anything happened to his father's car he'd be disowned and he drove on in silence.

Do you always talk to people as if you were slicing them with a knife? Harris Arden said. He flicked his ash out the window, his cigarette small in his hand.

The road took them through towns where rows of elms met overhead and threw blue shadows on the roofs. Clotheslines fluttered on upper porches, two boys fished in a river, steel cranes rose up above the docks at Bath. Off the road were signs for sea lavender, eel, fresh mackerel, live lobsters, blueberries, corn picked today and in a pickup truck a little girl selling jam and pies. The sky was bleached behind torn clouds. Ann wondered what it would be like to kiss his mouth. By Wiscasset the mudflats swirled and shimmered under the bridge and further on was a hillside scorched by

fire with black spindly trees. A man stood with his hands on his
hips staring at a barn door. An apple tree floated beside a yellow
farmhouse. Harris pointed to a wreath of flowers at a turn near
Thomaston and memorials on town greens were polished wedges
cut from local granite. They passed a church with a black door and
houses with fish-scale shingles and dormer windows and slate
roofs. Cement steps led up to brick storefronts with trucks parked
diagonally outside. Restaurants had orange claws over their doors
and drive-in dairies had children sitting backwards at picnic tables
eating soft ice cream. Motels were named Water's Edge, Light
House, Sea View, Moody's.

Ann had grown up on a street outside of Boston with sidewalks
and no lawns and spent summers on the South Shore and the air
feathering by the window now smelled of the sea and recalled her
childhood and long days on the beach. She felt far from that childhood sitting in the woody but the distance between her and it
seemed suddenly voluptuous and she wondered if it showed and if
the person beside her had any idea of the happiness and content-
ment which had so suddenly and surprisingly taken possession of her.

The birds were loud in the morning then loud again at night just
before evening. A few chirps then silence, then a long trill. She
heard a car door slam and hum by below on Emerson Street. A dog
barked and was answered by another dog closer. The plumbing ran
at the far end of the hall and a heaviness filled her as the pain
moved in.

What are you doing?

It's going to storm. I'm closing the windows.

No, leave them open.

It will drench the rug, said the nurse, turning back, leaving them
up.

I want the air. Nothing like the air of a storm.

The suitcase had belonged to her mother, it had a smooth shel-
lacked surface with yellow stitching underneath the glaze. The

locks snapped and the corners were rounded, hollow and shell-like. Ann Lord could almost taste the surface of it at the back of her throat.

A warm July wind, the smell of a fish cannery. She stood beside him as the water went by. His shirt collar was bent under, but she didn't untuck it. His hair was wheat-colored and unruly and shook like cotton tufts in the wind. The engine of the ferry vibrated through the railing and Ann Grant felt it in her hands and chest. Being a doctor he was not a lot outdoors and his face didn't have the same color as the other passengers'. He told her about the emergency room being busy on full moons, he told her people trusted doctors more than they should.

Ann felt the excitement of the wedding, of the people traveling, of the suitcases opening and cheeks kissed and the new dresses and the cocktails and dinners and suits needing to be pressed. She'd first visited the Wittenborns' when she was fifteen after meeting Lila that winter at skating class in Boston and knew well the flowered chairs of the living room and the routine of taking picnics made by Mrs. Babbage to Butter or Fling or Coleman's Island, traveling in crowded motorboats and landing with care on rocky beaches and while it had been new and different to her at first she now felt a part of it. The man beside her added a new element. She did not know what to expect from him and everything he said surprised her. She imagined he would always surprise her.

As they came in the channel he asked her about the island and she pointed to the boathouse moving past them on the shore and told him she'd first kissed a boy there. It was not the sort of thing she usually told anyone and immediately tried to cover it up by telling about the parties they'd go to with bonfires and people falling from rafters and the time Buddy drove an outboard over the floats. They came in sight of town and she saw the grey general store with the bulletin board encased in glass and the stone wall where the island boys smoked and the gas pumps on the next dock with the fishing boats and the ferry landing where people stood now waving.

She spotted Lila wearing pigtails and little white shorts and Carl beside her, solid in big white shorts. They already looked married the way they stood side by side waving, not needing to look at each other or to touch.

Ann waved back, Harris Arden didn't. She glanced at his mouth and from this angle saw a split in his bottom lip which gave her a pleasant rattled feeling which did not go away when the ferry docked and they bumped the pilings and Harris Arden picked up her yellow suitcase along with his bag and was still there when they kissed Lila and Carl hello.

Gigi Wittenborn came running forward, barefoot, sunburnt, giving off a whiff of alcohol when Ann kissed her. Lila's sister Gigi was just twenty but taller than Lila.

They've been picnicking with the Holts, Lila whispered. You get the picture.

Two strapping Holt brothers hovered near Gigi, there were usually a few boys hovering around Gigi and her scattered beauty. Ann saw Harris Arden shake Gigi's hand and was relieved to see he didn't seem overly intrigued. Buddy peered over Gigi's shoulder looking into the cup she held, took it from her hand and drank the rest of it. The excited feeling increased in the gathering.

Ann had had feelings with a few other boys and with each there was something particular to the person which was unique and it seemed that the particular feeling around Harris Arden was more unique than usual. There was something larger in him, in his stillness, in the way he moved. She watched him carry the suitcases to the car not hurrying but purposeful and intent and sort of angry. He'd been playful with her during their drive but the way his body moved was not playful, it was big and impatient and final, like another continent. They loaded into the old station wagon. Harris Arden pulled off his sweater and his stomach showed. Ann saw it from where she was sitting in the back—his head was cut off by the roof, and the skin of his stomach was smooth.

Carl drove. The island roads were unchanged, always with a little curve, sometimes with a dip like a rollercoaster. Lila facing forward in the front related the news. Her mother was doing her
utmost to drive her insane, the Slaters were having them for a
cookout, her father was pretending nothing unusual whatsoever
was going on. Ann was staying in the guest cottage where the ice
box was filled with flowers, Harris Arden and Ralph were in the
main house. The tires rumbled over the wooden bridge at Bishops
Harbor then skidded at the unpaved turnoff to the Wittenborn
compound and clanged over the cattle guards ridged in the dirt.
They were packed into the car closely and Harris Arden's arm was
pressed alongside Ann's. The world was perfect and tight and balanced and as they drove past the sheep on the tilted field it seemed
that the trunk of each cedar tree was perfectly shaped and had
been set down in precisely the place it belonged.

A club thumped her back and a little fire burst into flame and
smoke ran through her. The smoke was orange.

Mother, they said. Mother.

She was being summoned, they were waiting downstairs. But
she hadn't prepared her statement. She pretended not to hear. It
was as if a thick bandage were wrapped over her eyes but she could
still see through. She heard them and heard herself but it was
much smaller what they said. Each word seemed sort of whittled
down while she felt oddly added onto. Her brain felt as big as the
ceiling. Meaning was slipping but she saw now meaning had always
been slipping off to the side only she hadn't noticed it before. She
stopped using certain words.

Sometimes she woke in the middle of the night and was
struck with a panic and dread so sudden and overwhelming her
heart stopped and she feared her nerves had seized up for good,
then somehow the moment passed and she was able to breathe
again.

✧

She felt his presence in the room as she showered before dinner. There was no one like him in the world. She thought of his doctor's hands.

The boys she'd been seeing in New York were fast-walking boys who held restaurant doors open and because there was so much to look at swiveled their heads around. They talked about themselves boldly or shyly and at the end of dinner would focus on her. Sometimes they reached for her hand. Sometimes she walked home with her hand still in theirs.

Ann Grant had had three beaux by then. Frank Fallon from Gray Gable Road was six years ago, and Malcolm Flynn in New York was the first real grownup. She'd been in love with Malcolm Flynn, at least she thought so till now. Now with this new feeling she looked back on Malcolm Flynn and wondered how she could have endured him for so long. *Forget Malcolm,* said Fiona Speed, rummaging through her purse. She turned to the man at the bar beside her and asked in a sweet high British accent for a cigarette then turned back to Ann with her low real voice. *Forget Malcolm,* she said. And Lila at the breakfast table behind Mr. Wittenborn's blooming orchid screwed up one eye, puzzled at Ann's fascination with this man. It doesn't sound as if he's being really fair. They didn't even know the extent of the humiliating scenarios, prone beside the unringing phone, consoling *him* for canceling the weekend at a Massachusetts inn. She could no longer confide in her friends, ashamed for needing his intermittent attentions and believing that the wind which blew down the icy sidewalks was more precious for being around him as he hurried along. She lost weight, drank coffee for lunch. *Forget Malcolm,* they said. *It doesn't look as if Malcolm is going to get married for a long time.*

He'd been a change from the boys at home who were good-natured and fun on the beach and kept you dancing all night but looked frightened when you wanted to talk. Frank Fallon was a dear and even fascinating for a while after she'd licked snow off his hot cheek. But Frank didn't have a clue about her, he went on to marry Kathleen McNamara and they already had five children.

She met Malcolm Flynn at a cocktail party. He walked right up to Ann and afterwards with a group out at dinner Malcolm sat beside her and spoke near her face and was lively and abrupt and slightly taut and when they slipped their coats on by the cashier he pulled her away and said, Now I want you all to myself, nearly carrying her out the door. He hailed a cab and whisked her downtown to a bar crowded with men in sleek haircuts and women in little black dresses and gloves. He knew the bartender, he knew people inching by, but his attention didn't stray from her beyond a stiff salute to passing figures. He ordered her a gimlet. He didn't talk overly about his job, the business side of magazines, but about trips he'd taken and ones he wanted to take. He asked her what she thought about things. She had never been the object of a campaign of this sort and within two weeks Malcolm Flynn had her in his thrall. The first night she stayed at his apartment she lay awake watching a red ambulance light loop across the ceiling, feeling grownup to be in New York sleeping in a man's bed. He had made her feel silly for holding onto her virginity and she saw now he was right. She'd needed to be coaxed. The next morning back in her tiny flat on Sixty-eighth Street changing out of her evening clothes for work she was aware of something darkening her sense of satisfaction. Soothed from the physical contact she dimly glimpsed through the haze of pleasure and vanity an image she didn't want to inspect too closely, an uneasiness about Malcolm Flynn's character. She wondered if he wasn't a little spineless. After those first weeks he never flooded her again with quite the same attention but maintained just enough exuberance now and then to keep her attached. Doubts about his character persisted. The trip to Florida to meet investors turned out to be the trip to Florida with the lingerie model from Bendel's. There was an episode with his best friend's sister during the Christmas holidays in Pittsburgh, which Ann wouldn't have known about if the poor girl hadn't rung her up in tears. But Malcolm's apologies came so sweetly in the new special quiet of their shared dark pillow and she thought this is what was meant by compromise in love. It was two years before Ann could extract herself.

Attempting to get away from him she often spent weekends visiting Lila in Cambridge and that's where Vernon Tobin appeared. Ann had always known Lila's cousin but suddenly he was five years older. He was working in a bank. His attitude to Ann was respectful, unlike Malcolm's. When she finally broke off with Malcolm, Vernon was there.

Vernon presented his own dilemma, one he suffered from more than Ann. He was good, but she did not love him.

Someone banged over the hollow threshold. It was Gigi, bright-eyed, with a slash of sunburn across her cheekbones.

Ann Ann Ann, Gigi said. Tell me who he is.

Ann blushed knowing right away whom she meant.

She felt better knowing he was there in the room.

Just give me your hand, she said. We wasted so much time.

I'll wait till he comes down, said Teddy's wife Lauren, sitting on the porch steps. Her twin daughters were asleep in the car and she positioned herself so she could keep an eye on them.

She's sleeping most of the time, Margie said.

He says she talks in her sleep.

She mumbles a lot, Constance said.

He says it's interesting.

Aunt Grace said she's quoting Carole Lombard movies or Duke Ellington songs.

Teddy thinks it's about her boyfriends, Lauren said.

Husbands is more like it, Constance said.

He says he's hearing more about her life than he ever did before. Lauren went taut, thinking she heard a sound from the car. No, she said to herself, and relaxed.

Like what? Margie said looking at Lauren with interest.

Constance hit Margie's chair. I doubt Mother has any deep dark secrets, she said.

# 4. Torches

In June the leaves were thin and light green and by August they would be dark and thick as fur *let's just say you won't see the leaves change this year.* Now it was July. She thought of the house beneath her. The marble table in the hall with the silver communion dish on feet and a drawer tangled with keys, a clay head sculpted by Margie. Then the hooks under the stairs and coats hanging. More coats in the closet. A row of flower prints on the wall. In the living room the fireplace mantle had a wooden crucifix from Mexico from her honeymoon with Ted and the twisted silver Stackpole candlesticks, one with a dent from the time Ted threw it *goddamn it Ann* and the French clock of Oscar's. On the floor a wire basket filled with magazines, on the bookshelf framed photos propped against crimson leather, gold letters, titles sideways, books in shelves up to the ceiling. With the lights out the living room hushed. The dining room, grey and white floor. Teddy and

Paul used to hide in the elephant ear plant, playing jungle. Once Paul bit a leaf. The chairs pushed tight around the table, the china basket in the center. In the pantry the cabinet latches painted thick, the cocktail glasses behind the glass, a glass ashtray with bubbles. No that was somewhere else. Then Ted's green coupe popped into her mind, it was in the driveway in Connecticut and she thought of the Connecticut house with the chestnut blossoms like suds on the gravel in the spring and the lawn littered with yellow leaves in the fall *let's just say you won't see* in the spring daffodils clustered down the sloping lawn then summer with the boats humming. They were eating under a pergola, but the light was European, there was bougainvillea and dappled shadows. A plate of red peppers in oil. The French nanny had a polka dot bathing suit and wore a ponytail. Little red flowers like trumpets poked through the trellis outside their bedroom. Ted was late coming back, he'd stopped for a drink. The water threw off a white light on the white sidewalk by the shops on the Riviera. Clouds blurred into pale blue. She had a straw bag and blue espadrilles. The children were eating dishes of ice cream with wafers pointing up. They were playing tag with the waves. She was waiting for Ted in the bar. *You are too lovely to sit alone* the man said. Ted was late. *Where were you? not this again* the white beach, the rusted hulk of the shipwreck on the shoals. She unfolded canvass chairs, Ted opened the umbrella. He stood at the bar with a towel around his waist. Constance wore a straw hat. Margie held a mainsail. They were in Maine, those were New England clouds. The beach was of stone and the picnic basket wicker. Cold chicken legs, lemonade from a thermos, Mrs. Babbage's cookies, the Cutlers' boat with the green cushions. Carl was pulling in the anchor. The boys were skipping stones. Someone passed out plates of cake, it was leftover birthday cake. Then her mother was standing in the doorway at Gray Gable Road. Her face powdered white, her lips purple. Ann sat on her father's lap, it was her birthday, the candles came in shining. Everyone was shining. She held the button of her father's shirt, he smelled like smoke. Other Grants were there, Aunt Joy and Uncle

Donny, and Mrs. Futter from next door in a flowered apron, the Jurgins with Lisel in a party dress. Ann was five, she felt it on her cheeks, sitting in her father's lap. They clapped when she blew out the flame. It was July. She turned and kissed her father. She had on a white dress of dotted Swiss! Her mother yanked her arm and pulled her up and sat her down in another seat. *Never kiss your father on the mouth* whispered, spitting. *Do you hear? Never.*

They were gathered on the public dock of Bishops Harbor loading into boats. Ann Grant spotted him as she came down the ramp. He had changed into a dark jacket. He was talking to Lizzie Tull, Lila's college friend and another bridesmaid who was small and wide-faced with a little tent of frizzed hair. He was hunched over adjusting himself to her level, his hands shoved in his pants pockets. Lizzie was babbling on the way she did with strangers and men and Ann was irritated to see Harris Arden responding with an open ingratiating expression. Up until then he'd seemed perfect.

Clint Stone, the boatman, sat at the helm of the *Happenstance*. Ann said hello wondering if he remembered her. She had not grown up around servants and wasn't sure of the protocol though she assumed there was one. Clint Stone tipped the brim of his cap, a Maine greeting which could mean anything.

The girls were dressed in pretty much the same thing, narrow cocktail pants, flat shoes, little shirts which buttoned up the back and cardigan sweaters which buttoned up the front. They differed in the small detail. Lila Wittenborn wore a charm bracelet, Lizzie Tull a pearl necklace. Lila's cousin Eve, her hair dyed platinum since Ann last saw her, had beaded embroidery on her sweater. Ann Grant who had a horror of uniforms was wearing a Mexican shirt.

They crossed the cove in two boats.

The evening water was glassy and dark green at the edges and bright in the middle with the setting sun. Ann Grant sat in the crafted wood of the *Happenstance* beside Mrs. Wittenborn who held a cut crystal cocktail glass rimmed with beet red lipstick.

I could strangle Dick for not letting us live in New York, she was saying. You must be loving it.

Ann admitted it was more exciting than Boston.

Lila sat in the stern beside her father, her thick hair not separating in the wind. She caught Ann's eye and they both smiled. The day after tomorrow, they were both thinking. Lila was the closest thing Ann had to a sister. The Wittenborns had taken in Ann as they did many people, hardly noticing. Mr. Wittenborn wore an ascot, blue blazer and captain's hat, his eyelids fluttered, gazing out with pity on the world. Lila held the top of her cardigan closed against the wind and put her head on her father's shoulder.

. . . Endlessly at the Stork Club, Mrs. Wittenborn was saying. She had married Mr. Wittenborn when she was seventeen and still looked as young as her daughters. The cocktail splashed out of her glass when the boat encountered some wake. Oops, she said unconcerned.

Harris Arden was in the other boat, the *Wild Goose.* His back was to Ann, sitting on the edge, and he was still listening to Lizzie Tull. A champion tennis player, she was demonstrating a stroke. Carl Cutler, the groom, was at the helm. Carl was the sort of responsible steady person you let drive your boats. He was quiet and determined with a plodding manner and at twenty-nine was a successful businessman operating on the principle that you didn't give in to personal likes, kept what made a profit and dropped what didn't. His affection was reserved exclusively for Lila and he showed a rare mooniness when you saw them holding hands. Ann Grant had never seen him flirt or even look with interest at another woman.

The high pitch of a speedboat's motor rose behind them, overtaking the quiet motoring boats. Heads in the *Happenstance* turned. A boat came whizzing by, its bow above the water's surface. At the helm was Gigi in a long turquoise dress, hair flying, standing on the driver's seat, bending down to the steering wheel. A chiffon scarf rippled from her neck.

Mrs. Wittenborn barely turned her chin to look, keeping her knees and shoulders facing forward. There goes your daughter, Dick, she said, sipping her cocktail. What has she got on?

Ann's mother had a similar attitude—what one wore was of vital importance.

It's the Holts' boat, said Mr. Wittenborn.

In the front a young man was flattened out on the cushions. The wake spread behind like a fish bone.

Mrs. Wittenborn muttered. Ann thought she heard, I can't do a thing about her, then thought it might be, I can't understand a thing about her.

The motor ground like a chain saw.

Who's with her, Kevin or Joe? Mr. Wittenborn had an odd way of talking, with little catches in his voice.

I think Kevin, Lila said. She'd witnessed so many catastrophes with her sister her attitude was one of jaded alarm.

Gigi cried across the water. I'm writing Lila and Carl!

Must be in script, said Lila, long suffering.

Gigi jerked the wheel to turn and fell off the chair.

Dick, said Mrs. Wittenborn.

Mr. Wittenborn frowning took a deep breath. Clint Stone reached for the throttle and eased it back, not needing direction. When the *Happenstance* was slowed down, Mr. Wittenborn stood up.

Above the idling motor he shouted. That's enough!

Gigi wasn't even looking in their direction, scrambling up to the controls, delighted to be scaring herself. Ann noticed something glinting around her neck which looked very much like the diamond necklace Mr. Wittenborn had given Mrs. Wittenborn when after two daughters she bore him a son. (The girls had been celebrated with pearls.) Mrs. Wittenborn was taking advantage of the diminished wind to light a cigarette.

Gigi! Mr. Wittenborn insisted. Gigi!

The statuesque figure was back at the wheel. She struck a pose with an arm flung back. Her hair was the same light brown color as her skin and her teeth at a distance were very white. She'd been striking the same pose since Ann Grant had first met her at age ten, with her jagged bangs across one eye. The A is the hardest! she screamed.

Jesus, came from Lila under her breath.

Kevin Holt had his arms braced against the railing, his smile tight with fear. Then the boat tilted so sharply you could see the floor and Gigi became a blue star with arms and legs extended and they all watched helplessly as she pitched over the stern.

Mrs. Wittenborn jumped up, spilling her drink on Ann. Now she's overboard for godsakes! Clint! The throttle revved. The *Wild Goose* was closer and Carl got there first and before anyone knew what was happening a large figure had shed his dark jacket and leapt off into the tranquil water and was swimming toward Gigi's bobbing head. His arms plowed the water in long pulling strokes. My God, thought Ann, watching Harris Arden, he's a hero too.

The motorboat turned into a fly, passing her face. She brushed at it but it was gone. Someone sat on her chest. The fly turned into a lawnmower out the window. Grass grew on the pillow beside her. She could feel a man in the room.

Who's there?

Hello, Ann. It's Oliver. Ollie Granger's voice always had a little heft of pleasure in it.

Have you completed your mission? she said.

Not quite, he answered right away.

The A is the hardest part.

Yes it is.

I have an Indian princess in my mouth, she said.

That sounds right, said Ollie Granger.

We didn't need lights.

No, we didn't. A look of concern came over Oliver Granger's face.

With no change in her tone Ann Lord went on, When are you going back to Maine? Is Lily up?

She's there now.

Tell me about all the dinner parties I'm not missing in the least.

One after the other, said Ollie Granger.

❊

Torches on poles lit up the open deck of the Slaters' house which jutted out over jagged rocks. Helping themselves to chicken and potato salad the guests talked about the accident till Gigi and Harris Arden appeared after a half hour changed into dry clothes and since no one was hurt there was a lot of joking and teasing. Ann Grant was approaching Harris Arden when she saw Gigi, now in a yellow shift, the necklace returned to her mother's jewelry case, bend forward parting her hair to show what might be a bump and Harris Arden examining it doctor-like then saying something to Gigi who laughed and looked up at him with what could only be described as adoration. Ann veered off. When she took her plate she carried it to a bench at the far end of the dock beneath a pyramid of geraniums opposite the little group which had formed around the hero.

Buddy Wittenborn edged over to make room for Ann.

She was embarrassed she'd had any feeling for the person. He was in her sights and she couldn't help watching him and soon she developed the idea that he wanted to be talking to her as well and for that very reason was staying away. A little circle of devotees had gathered around him, the girls with glazed looks, the boys tilting their ears, even Mrs. Slater with her stiff neck and white hair was giggling now and then. Ann glanced over, hardly listening to the ongoing controversy about the bridesmaids' jackets. Lizzie was lobbying for, Ann had cast her vote against, the small shoulders did not look right on her. Gail Slater, Lila's oldest friend, also a bridesmaid, looked alert and interested and maintained neutrality. Buddy silently buttered his corn. Harris Arden had changed into one of Buddy's shirts, red and white striped with a monogram, a shirt Buddy would wear only if forced. He balanced a plate on his knees and his long legs made the plate higher than anyone else's. He held a chicken leg with one bite taken out and stared at Eve Wittenborn's painted mouth as she talked (Lila's cousin though a bridesmaid was not enough of the inner circle to be consulted). Despite her new look of a movie star Eve Wittenborn remained earnest and dull. When she stopped talking only then did Harris Arden take another bite of his food. Ann glanced away, feeling she'd looked too long, and as Lila was saying frankly she was sick of discussing it and they should wear what they wanted, the image stayed with her of him with his wet hair closer around his head and of his drumstick hovering in the air and his mouth parted listening.

There was a commotion across the deck, Ann saw Gigi fall onto Harris Arden's chest calling him my hero. Everyone laughed and Ann hated him. He recoiled a little from Gigi despite looking down at her bare legs as she crossed them. Then his gaze moved down to the wooden planks and traveled out across the deck and rose and stopped landing on Ann.

Her first instinct was to look away. He was staring straight at her. She struggled to look back. His eyes without the dark glasses covering them had something merry in them, though she could not read their intent. How was he looking at her? Curious? No. She returned the stare. Here I am. She tried to maintain that. Here I am. Her heart was crashing. Neither smiled. She felt as if the whole factory of herself had been thrown into operation with one switch. Who would look away first? His mouth was closed with the teeth crowded behind it, the dent in his lip made a shadow. Everything had a different position without anything having moved. She saw it all from a different angle. His eye had a spark of light in it. She couldn't look anymore, she looked away.

The air was trembling then it was as if a telescope brought everything into vivid focus and she felt the scallop shape of the geranium leaves and the smooth slivered wood of the weathered seats and the air where her shirt bloused out not touching her skin. A figure passed by and the shadow slid over her. Behind the spruce trees came the snap of the flag flown when the family was in residence. She felt the snap in her spine.

Gigi clinked her glass with a fork. The talk stopped and everyone turned. Here's to my sister Lila, she said, standing up on the bench and raising a glass. Her voice was as husky as if she'd been smoking cigarettes since she was three. Lila is . . . Lila's great. Everyone loves Lila. She paused. But no one as much as I do.

A low disembodied voice came out of the darkness beside Ann Grant. Except, said the voice of Lila's brother, me.

*       *       *

The door clicked shut.

Too bad you can't crawl in with me, she said.

Wouldn't that be nice.

I'm not the same. Needless to say.

He took her hand. Your hand is still the same. The same old hand.

Same old, she said.

The same young one, I should say.

Thank you. That's nice of you.

The same sweet hand.

Very nice.

She looked across the room to all the things which had come to her over the years and by now ought to give her some satisfaction. The inkwell nestled in a bronze bird's nest, the primitive oil of a church she'd found in that junk shop, the French enamel saucers with the fly pattern . . . they would last and not she. Is this what she would leave behind? The things in the house were not herself. The children would be left and they had come from her but they were not herself either. Nothing was herself but what had happened to her and the only place that was registered was inside. And even that was a kind of vapor.

You're being quiet today, he said.

Just thinking.

He let her think for a while.

Then she said, I won't ask you.

Ask me what?

If it was the same.

What?

For you.

Ann.

I mean, if it mattered as much. I don't know why I . . . really . . . why I go on about it.

You can go on about it.

Yes. She laughed. That's just it. I could. She thought for a while more and when she spoke seemed to address herself more than him. But why bother?

So I'll know? he said.

She looked at his face. She could still see the face she'd first seen in him though now it was older. She could still see it. She smiled. You can never know, she said.

❖   ❖   ❖

She communed with herself in the Slaters' bathroom needing a pause in the socializing. On the wall was a framed cartoon of a woman kissing her husband's golf balls and a caption saying that would make his putter rise. The grey and red curtains with kettles on them were faded nearly white between the folds and torn near a rusty hook and a green stain made a leaf shape in the sink. The Slaters were not poor. Lila had said that in New England the rich let old things stay old.

When she came out through the low-ceilinged living room Harris Arden was coming in the doorway, stepping in sideways. He was too big to step in straight. He crouched, accustomed to stooping through doorways, and his features picked up a sharp shadow from a yellow lamp and she saw a new expression of being inwardly lit up from talking to people, sort of fortified by the attention. So he had that expression too.

He walked toward her with his long legs. A cone of light was thrown onto the wall from a lampshade painted with nautical flags. His tall legs kept coming toward her. The windows had black panes with glints of light. She watched him walking toward her again and again. Laughter came from outside. She smiled. He half-smiled back. Doubt swept through her. He was mysterious and the otherness of his life suddenly struck her. She wanted to be thrown onto his back and hauled off. She wondered how warm his skin was or how cool or how soft at the throat. She wanted to climb around on him. She looked at his arms and wondered what they'd do with a girl. He seemed to have a thousand decisions made inside him and many secrets and she wanted to know what they were and to study him and watch the secrets change. She wanted, she wanted. She felt drowsy and alert at the same time. In the long time of crossing the room as they neared one another among the squeaking wicker chairs and the model boat encased in glass and the straw rug, it struck her that he would not be here long, their time was limited and perhaps she ought to do something and be more forward but then she thought they had found each other. There was a glass-topped bamboo table in the middle of the room in front of a sofa making the space narrow and as they reached it at the same time Ann Grant knocked its corner jarring a bowl of sea glass. He caught her elbow.

Careful, he said. And he gripped her arm.

He might just as well have lifted her slowly into the air and flung her up against the wall or slapped her across the face or tripped her and thrown her onto the floor.

She sidestepped him with a bright look and opened the door onto the deck and the summer night and the low voices and was glad for the darkness. She had a smile plastered across her face. She tried to stop it and found she could not. God she thought this is ridiculous. It was what her mother might have said and a curious thing to say to herself since ridiculous was the opposite of what she believed this was.


Constance stood at the bureau picking things up.

I ought to tell you about the will, said Ann Lord.

Constance dropped the top back on a jade jar. Margie stopped hugging her knees and put her feet on the floor. At the window Teddy turned his head but kept his body facing out.

You don't have to, Teddy said.

She can if she feels like it, Margie said.

Obviously she feels like it if she's bringing it up, said Constance.

You can address me directly, said the woman on the bed. I am still here.

I don't care about the will, Teddy said into the glass.

*Will you leave the light on?* their feet pattering above her *I can hear you up there* the glass chandelier on the table shaking *back in bed right now!*

It's being divided up among the four of you, you and Nina, so I hope you'll care a little. And the little girls and of course Julian.

Constance stood over the chest at the foot of the bed. So we shouldn't expect anything unusual? she said, wanting to end the discussion. *Will you read it again just one more time*

I don't know what you expect, said her mother.

Constance's face twisted a little and she left the room.

Did I say something?

Teddy followed after her.

What's the name of the one at night? said Ann Lord.

What? said Margie. Oh you mean Nurse Homans.

I don't like her.

She doesn't seem too bad.

I want to get rid of her.

Mother, why?

Shall I get Constance to do it?

No, I'm just wondering why.

I told you, I don't like her.

No reason?

Margie's little arms around her neck were strangling her *don't go Mother don't go please* Ann tried to stand up and her legs wobbled lifting the two of them *you're always going*

I'll get Constance to take care of it.

No, I will. I just wanted to know a good reason.

There is no good reason. Don't waste your life waiting for good reasons, Margie. You'll wait and wait.

Now she had that terrible look on her face. *When are you com-*

*ing back? Why can't I come?* She should not have had children, she did not know how to answer their eyes. She tried to think of something to say. The ceiling was there with its uneven plaster.

I'm a writer now, she said.

Margie leaned forward, her expression changed. What?

She pointed up. My blank page.


Charlie Elisophen's fiancée was describing the terrible heat in Malaysia where she grew up. They were sitting on a stone wall below the terrace. Ann had left a space between her and Harris Arden. Buddy lay on the grass looking up at the sky and Carl's friend Monty had such pale hair it seemed to glow in the dark. Harris Arden asked her about the colonists and she shrugged and said the whole thing was much simpler than people thought and over-emphasized here and the natives didn't really want to govern themselves and it was not really something you could understand if you hadn't lived there. Harris said he had been there but guessed not long enough. Buddy who hadn't appeared to be listening said, I don't suppose there's anyone here to speak for the natives.

Lizzie Tull's silhouetted bushy head came bouncing down the lawn. She plopped herself down beside Harris Arden and began interrogating him. Ann listened to many of the same questions she'd asked, feeling she at least knew him better, but was sorry she'd not been as enthusiastic as Lizzie since Harris was smiling at her exclamations.

So if you're so perfect, Lizzie said, why aren't you married?

Ann braced herself for the answer which was eclipsed by a rocket whistling off the porch followed by a crack. They were shooting off Roman candles. Lizzie jumped up first and the others followed. Buddy crawled up the little slope on his hands. Ann stood, Harris Arden stayed sitting. She didn't move. They'd not exchanged a word all night.

Are you having a good time? he said in a quiet voice.

Sure.

How are you?

It seemed one of the more intimate things anyone had ever said to her.

Fine. She sat back down beside him. That was quite a rescue tonight.

I thought she might have hit her head. That would have been bad. Head injuries are not good.

It scared me for a minute, Ann said. Gigi gets in a lot of trouble.

She's an interesting person, he said.

Gigi was often the subject of conversation. Gigi had gotten arrested, a boy had climbed up to her window, she cracked up the car. But Ann had never heard anyone refer to her as an interesting person.

Later she and Harris Arden took back the putt-putt he'd brought Gigi in after the accident. She sat on the plank in the middle holding her sandals with his sweater wrapped shawl-like around her and her bare feet cooled by the sheet of water sliding front to back in the bottom.

Do you know about boats? she said as he stepped into the stern.

Not at all. He pulled the cord and nothing happened. He pulled again and it started.

There's a safety light, she said.

We don't need a light. There's a moon.

She felt content with him steering behind her. The wind was soft on her face. The water was still and lights from the houses onshore made little paths of pleated light coming down.

You look like an Indian princess, he said.

She didn't know what to say to that.

Do you prefer a full moon? he said. Or a half?

I like them both. Then she remembered. But one is always better?

Yes.

Sometimes it doesn't matter, she said.

His voice was nearly blotted out by the humming motor. Everything matters, he said.

If there had been a part of her not in thrall with him that part was now gone.

❀   ❀   ❀

Well it doesn't matter now, she said.
  Of course it does.
  It did . . .
  It still matters, he said.
  How can it? How can it matter anymore?
  It matters inside, he said.
  Where's that? Can we go there together?
  In a way.
  She was silent. They looked at each other in silence.

❀   ❀   ❀

Leaning into the deep sill of the screened window they faced the dark lawn and the bay beyond. The group on the flowered sofas was behind them, Lila with tea and Carl's arm around her, Ralph with ankles crossed telling about the latest wedding, his twelfth time as an usher. Kevin Holt mixed drinks with Gigi at the leather bar cart.
  Back there you had an expression on your face. It made me want to kiss you.
  He was very close so she didn't turn her head but her eyes shifted in his direction.
  Are all the boys in Chicago like you?
  Sure, we're all over the place.
  Ann looked out and saw a figure on the lower lawn. At first she thought it was one of the men working on the tent then saw it was Buddy. He walked by without glancing toward the house. His shirttails were out. It was like him to be wandering around in the night leaving lost things behind him. Buddy held loosely onto things. She felt a wave of affection for him, having affectionate feelings in abundance.

There's a rock garden down there, she said, feeling bold.

Is there?

You want to see?

He pushed back from the sill. Without turning to the others they opened the screen door to the long porch and went out. At another time Ann would have glanced back to the girls. This was different. This was hers.

# 5. THE ROCK GARDEN

They came in one after another, up the stairs on the pale-green nailed carpet around the flat top of the landing past the prints of ships sailing through icebergs and ships aflame at night, past the black framed photographs in the hall of Ann Katz on a zebra banquet wearing satin straps and thick bracelets, Margie and Constance in bathtub suds, the twins holding fishing poles, Ted stepping out of a plane cockpit, Ann in riding boots by a tent, Oscar and Ann on the terrace, little Paul with a parrot on his shoulder . . . they glided into her room and stood underwater holding their breaths watching her breathe water staying very still till finally they could leave, get out and gulp air.

They entered fearful, some were better at hiding it than others.

Mrs. Storey brought her dog who set his head on the bed next to Ann Lord's limp hand. Hello old girl, she said coming in, and Good-bye old girl, when she left.

Mrs. Roland, Elsie's eighty-eight-year-old mother, came up with a cane wearing a purple skirt above her stick legs. You're beginning to look Oriental, she told Ann. You'll be fine, she said, and thumped her knee. Ann said, I know.

They came to her bedside and talked about what was going on downstairs, out the door, out on the street, in other houses, out in the world. It had been hot that weekend, it didn't rain in Dover but did in Beverly Farms. The beach was glorious. Camilla Shepley was getting married again, Penny Montgomery's wedding in New Orleans was going to be enormous and she was organizing the whole thing. Nina was arriving on Friday, she had the second lead in this play, something about kids on the street in Brooklyn. Lila Cutler hoped to get down from Maine but her back was bad. The traffic on the way over was terrible, the Square was a mess. The Eastmans had telephoned and so had Mrs. Beegin and Mrs. Brocaw and Mrs. Weld and Dan Shepley. *What else?* they said, *What else?* There was an interesting article, they'd seen something stupid on TV, what was the movie they wanted to see? They'd had dinner at the Whites', they were still not talking to the Brocaws, Peach Howe was visiting from Florida, she'd definitely had a lift, Ollie Granger had won the race with the Hallowells, they'd brought her a pillowcase from Kit Eastman's store, Jared Brocaw punched out the starter at the golf course, there was a wonderful Winslow Homer exhibit at the MFA they'd not been to yet. Ann Lord listened propped against the pillow following the movement when a person entered and put down a vase on a surface which up until then had never seen a vase or picked up a newspaper before sitting down in a chair or leaned a briefcase by the door or turned on the lamp in the corner when it started to get dark.

Someone held the cup while she tried to clamp her lips onto the straw but the straw swiveled away. A hand came forward to help and she waved it away, what else did she have to do but fumble with a straw? Everyone went silent and she had to say, Go on I'm listening, and continued fumbling, as if nibbling air. They did their best to talk on *what else? let's see* but kept watching till her lips clamped onto the straw and she drew up a sip of lemonade and they could heave a sigh of relief. *What else?* It was important that someone always be talking otherwise the silence took hold like a Virginia creeper invading a garden and darkened the air with what was going on in the room, the battle with pain, the downhill journey. It was not discussed that they were all here to see her off. They brought in bits of the world and when there was silence the absurdity of conversation was too apparent.

They knew how to get up in the morning and drive the car to work, to organize carpools, roast a chicken, cut back the roses, have a baby, dress the children, mix a cocktail, hoist a jib, dance a foxtrot, order in French, balance the checkbook, but they did not know so well how to do this. Sometimes she looked at them and thought not unkindly they're just jumping over puddles.


He must have a girlfriend. There must be someone back in Chicago. There was no one she could ask but Carl and she didn't want to ask Carl. She could have asked Harris Arden himself as they stepped into the night. The moon passed in and out of clouds and the grass was wet and her sandals were wet through in the thick grass. A path cut into a field of high grass making edges like a box. She went first and he followed, she did not turn around or ask him anything. She felt him behind with his light-colored eyes and his half-light hair and his skin blending in with the night. She didn't want to know more. They arrived at a place where the stones made steps leading down and she gestured with her arm and he grabbed her hand and pulled it to his ribs tucking it under, clamping down his arm and not letting hers go. They took careful steps pretending to concentrate on their feet but she was thinking of their arms and their hands. She floated in the darkness on his arm. They stepped awkwardly and slowly. She took a step too short and laughed and he steadied her. They inched along, feeling their way through the darker trees, bumping into each other.

She smelled marigolds, she smelled pine. The grass sloped and her eyes grew accustomed to the dark. They reached the clearing at the end of the path, she could make out the shapes of light-colored rocks and light-colored flowers in clusters and the darker edges near the ground under bushes. She let go of his hand and he kept his arm on her shoulder loosely. She stayed near him to keep his arm there sort of balancing so he wouldn't move. She felt odd standing in the center of the rock garden lawn not moving.

He was relaxed touching her and must be used to girls, she thought, and therefore he must have a girlfriend. If there was a girl she was probably a strong independent girl back in Chicago, strong-minded, a girl who made something of herself. Some great girl. But did the girl slice into him? If Ann asked and found out about a girl there was a good chance he would take his arm away, his arm which she liked having there. There was a good chance she would then step aside which she did not want to do. If she learned about some other girl it would stop the thing mounting between them, and to Ann this mounting thing felt colossal.

She ought to do something. What should she do? They were standing in the middle of the garden on the grass. Any minute he might remove his arm. She didn't want that, didn't want his arm to move away. She took hold of his hand dangling from her shoulder. Holding his hand like that felt peculiar as if someone else were doing it and after a moment she let go. There's a bench here some-where, she said, and turned and when she turned he pulled her back toward him. Ann, he said. His other arm came up so both arms were around her and her face was close to his chest. Ann, he said over her head. Ann. The way he said her name sent a thrill through her. It was even more thrilling than the way his arms felt. Her cheek was against his shirt and she could feel the warmth of his skin through the cotton. He was running his finger under the gathered elastic of her shirt at the neck and he pulled it back and bent and kissed her skin. Wait, she smiled. What? He didn't stop and she felt his lips. They made small noises. It's just—she began, still smiling and he buried his face in her neck making her smile more. She pulled back slightly, wasn't it too fast? this is where they were supposed to be going but her heart was beating too fast. Wait, she said, and put her hand on his chest. What is it. He was not worried, he was already further than she, he was already further along. Nothing, she laughed, but do I know you? He kissed her neck, his hair brushed her face. Yes, he murmured. He pulled her up to him. You do. I do? His hair went across her lips, she reached up to touch his head and was surprised how soft his hair was. You don't mind, he said. Do you. She could not answer. A force whirled through her. Who is he, she thought as a warm languor swept through her. Who is this Harris Arden? What was the house like where he lived. What did he think of and where were the streets he walked every day. What were these arms. Who did he know and what other girls did he kiss and where did he go.

Do you know, he said, how good you feel.

His hand at the back of her neck slipped under her shirt and slipped down her back. His hand on her skin. Do you mind? he said. He was smooth, he knew how to touch. She realized it with a little contraction inside, someone so smooth might not know how much it means, his hair in her face was darker than the night, the sky was light above the trees, all of it formed around the two of them, encasing them. He was taller than Ann and needed to crouch around her and when he stood up straight he lifted her in a tight grip nearly breaking her. She felt weak, she relaxed against him, his arms held her up. She had a sudden overpowering urge to lie down.

Still it seemed fast. His arms around her were lovely, but she didn't know where she was, his hand was reaching down her spine. Harris, she said. What? His hand moved further down.

She pulled back and looked at him. His face was so close. Isn't this strange?

Is it? His fingers tidied her hair.

Yes, it's strange.

No, it's nice, he said. You're nice.

The sky was grey stone with blurred clouds and the dark hill across the water was a sleeping animal stretched out. Her sandals were wet, she felt his skin under his shirt. How long did they stand there? Around them flat shapes had no color, only shades of grey and black. He pulled her shirt down off one shoulder then off the other and looked at her shoulders bare.

Stay like that always, he said.

He held out his jacket wing-like and enveloped her in it. Ann Ann Ann, he said. She was full of words but couldn't speak, she thought without fear, where are we going? feeling her shirt off her shoulders, huddled against him, waiting, knowing there was something dangerous. He had not even kissed her mouth. She waited, protected by his coat, thinking, he is taking me somewhere, where will it be? She went along.

Other embraces came vaguely back to her. It happened involuntarily, she was not thinking of other men but they appeared, others she'd touched, conjured up by this touching, the others she'd kissed in dark city living rooms with a yellow light glowing in the sky, the ones she'd hugged at the bottom of her stoop, Frank Fallon's head was being cradled in the front seat of his car, Malcolm's arm was around her in a cab. The faces appeared alongside this swooning feeling, lips on her neck being a most particular sensation and therefore recalling the other particular feeling of other lips. The images kept coming, vague and scattered, and she thought, how could one's life keep going this way? with more and more images piling up in one's heart and crowding and swelling like music. How was one to make room and to keep all of them? The answer which Ann Lord knew now having lived a life was that one did not. Things were forgotten. An astonishing amount of what one had known simply disappeared.

❀   ❀   ❀

You said it would always be there, she said. How could it?

He didn't answer right away. Once something's happened it is there. It can't be taken away. Nothing can change that.

Even if it doesn't last?

It lasts in your memory, he said. Is that nowhere?

It will be soon enough. She smiled.

Don't say that.

I can say anything. That's one thing about this. I can say anything now.

And you couldn't before? Were you so careful?

I didn't think so, she said. But it looks as if I was more careful than I thought.

He did not speak.

One thing though, everyone suddenly looks so brave.

Do they?

Yes. They know it doesn't last and yet . . .

And yet what?

They all carry on as if it did.

❖   ❖   ❖

She removed the sharp black teeth imbedded in her side. It's where the cancer was.

She'd not had a great deal of physical pain in her life, it had been saved up for the end. Childbirth had been overwhelming and like nothing else but she got the babies out of it, the babies who looked at her with a complete look, rolling on the grass slightly damp with spring, lying across her chest like a prize. She felt their tiny heartbeats, their fine hair against her lips, rubbing their fingers going a little cold, closing her eyes to the sun bright on her eyelids.

But the worst of it was *where is the water* what the weakness did to her thoughts *help me God* she could not push it away *God.* She had always been sure there was a God, she'd been taught by nuns, went to church, she used to go more. She did not doubt God, nor wanted to. Well she would find out in not too long a time. Had she been good enough in her life? Her fingers lay on the bedspread looking longer and thinner than they ever had. It was not a question she wanted to ask herself. It did not make the pain go away.

A door slammed in the draft down the hall, rattling the bottles on the bedside table. Ted's footsteps used to shake the floor from downstairs, rattling things, rattling things in her, she braced herself for his coming up. So much of life was bracing oneself *make it go away* she was not as she once was *I can't begin to explain* the old way was not working, she was apart behind a glass pane, her thoughts were splintered in her cheek, she was not gone yet *wait wait there's something* she wanted to be scattered she told them that, she thought dizzyingly of all the lives which had disappeared before her and how vast that was, she mustn't think of it, it was too tremendous to think of, too tremendous and awful, she tried folding herself back, a tune played in her head *don't get around much anymore* she just wanted it to go away *spring will be a little late this year* the light came in the window *let's just say you won't see the leaves* it was dark around her ankles, he was braiding her hair into the wet grass, it was still out of sight, the end of the road, the disappearance of herself, it was out of sight, she could not picture it, her imagination could not find it, herself not there *I'll never get out now* she thought *I'll never get back down those stairs* a moth batted against the ceiling against the ceiling against the ceiling

She sat at the dressing table in a white slip, screwed on pearl earrings, plucked her eyebrows. She blotted fuchsia lipstick, crossed the carpet in stocking feet. The girls were folding themselves into the closet mirrors. Phil was gone, they'd just gotten Abbott, they were living in Elsie Roland's carriage house. *Where are you going Mummy? Why are you always going out? When are you coming back?* There was someone the Rolands wanted her to meet. His name was Bill somebody. But Bill had brought a friend—Ted Stackpole. I'm going to marry that girl, Ted Stackpole said to the Rolands when Ann Katz left the room. He was big, filling his armchair, and rich. He did not need to work. Ted Stackpole liked to play games. Two weeks later he was carrying her off a porch away from the music. I have decided, he told her. Was it too soon? Don't think, said her friends, just do it. They took a honeymoon. The girls stood in the hall affronted watching her count her bags. Abbott lured them back into the kitchen. *We can make fudge!* In Mexico the gondolas were covered with flowers. They went through the tunnel twice. There was a lost lamb outside a cave and inside thrones and asparagus. He bought her earrings and a blouse and a crucifix. They drank mango wine and the windows swung wide open in the morning. Ann watched him walk naked from the bed.

They bought the house in Connecticut with the lawn stretching down to the water. There was a playhouse for the girls. They heard gulls cawing. They walked along the sea wall, raked leaves. At night it was black and quiet. Margie slept with the cat. There was a blizzard one spring. The eaves dripped. She planted tulips. On grey afternoons the vacuum hummed. A kite speared the ground like a dart. The girls were sprawled on the Sunday papers reading the funnies. She got a too short haircut. They shot clay pigeons, they shot ducks. They pulled her onto the bed. *I will always, I will never* The girls listened to her round belly. *When is it coming? How does it get out?* Constance wanted a brother, Margie wanted a brother too. *When is it coming out?* There were going to be two! Both boys. Ted had twins in his family. The scar would only show in a low bathing suit. He wasn't there when she woke up, he had gone for a drink. When he came he kept his coat on. She could tell the babies apart, but that had happened yesterday, having the twins.

Ted called her from upstairs. He called her from downstairs. Her life was checking off a list while he called. She changed diapers while he was calling. She fastened a bracelet against her rib. She tucked in the girls. *When are you coming back? One more kiss* She opened the window an inch, she left a crack of light in the door. She picked lint from their sweaters. Picked up the groceries. Picked out the fabric. Picked them up at school. Picked flowers. *What did you do today? What did you do? Because you're my wife that's why.* She ordered the liquor store to deliver *Ann come here! Ann! Ann!* She followed them down the dock. Followed them into the dining room. She fried bacon. She followed them into the darkness. They were at the office, they were playing golf. The children rode on their shoulders. They threw balls. She was in a box in the window. *Nothing's the matter why?* They mixed drinks. *Would you like another?* She never turned to another place, she never turned away. *Come here they said.* She was their wife. *Come here.* They handed back the baby. It was crying. Someone was always crying. *I'll go see* She laughed when he did the snaps up wrong.

She went shopping. The girls picked out shoes. She lay clothes on beds, tucked them into drawers. She was not in any other life only this one. She folded towels, sponged counters, wiped stoves, opened the icebox, set out tea cups, poured sugar bowls, baked potatoes, made hamburgers. They took it in front of the television. She had her hair done *you look nice tonight thank you* their hand pressed the small of her back, they played Beethoven's Ode to Joy, she wept, they drove home *is anything the matter I'm just tired that's all we're all a little tired* She slept on the left side, she slept on the right depending on which one it was. *I'm sorry not now I'm trying to tell you! Alright I'm listening* She lost what she meant, she could not find it, he was shouting. He was not saying *I will always I will never* He was furious. He was screaming. He pushed her down. He hit her on the back. *Goddamn you don't you ever*—no it could not have happened to her, that was someone else *because you're my wife that's why* She ran a bath. They were expected at dinner, ice dropped in glasses, red meat bled on plates, bright eyes in candlelight *you looked like you had a good time* She was in bed in the dark. *Come over here there you are*

She played tennis with the ladies. They lunched at the club— little white dresses, anklets with balls above the sneakers, bamboo sunglasses, bamboo pocketbooks. Four iced teas. Someone was putting in a new pool. Club sandwiches. Cottage cheese. Someone had a new sitter. Let's split a dessert. Someone was going back to Bermuda. Someone spent the night in New York. Have you read—? Have you seen—? She threw a sweater over her shoulders. Some- times there were bruises and in the morning Ted smelled of alcohol and rotten fruit. She did not mention it, they complained about their husbands, but she was quiet. She wished.

Then it happened. It was a spring morning. They called her from the club and she drove straight to the hospital. The tennis pro

met her there. Ted had played three sets then resting in the club-
house on a bench slumped to the side knocking over the cage of
tennis balls. The pro knew CPR. He called the ambulance. She listened to this story at the hospital and Ted was already gone. He left
her but she had already left him. She did not mention that. She had
wished for it and it had happened.

The morning of the funeral the water off the lawn was whipped
up chalk-grey. The twins were too young to go. The girls stood
beside her in Florence Eisemann dresses. People stood in the pulpit and said he lived how he wanted. Ted, they said, was saving
them a stool at the bar. She felt minutely defined, full of air, lighter
than air. Everyone came back to the house, it was like Thanksgiv-
ing with everyone in dark clothes, the women in heels. She felt hollow with a jaw of bronze. She could not sleep in their bed, could
not sleep, the air inside her was twisting around. They gave her
pills and finally she slept on the carpet. She did not know what to
do. She thought *I must do something* She became someone else.
There were the children. Grace Stackpole came and stayed. She
felt she had to decide something but there wasn't anything to
decide. There was nothing to do but to wait. That was all she could
do—wait to see what would happen, wait she supposed for someone else.

They stood for a long time in the rock garden meeting each other's
bodies for the first time too shy to stop standing and find the bench
Ann Grant had mentioned.

They stood and each time he touched a new place she sort of fell
off an edge and each time he said something she dropped deeper
into herself and further into the night around them. She would
have fallen over if he'd not held her up. Her hand was on his shoulder and she thought, this is his shoulder with my hand on it. He
had a sort of mirthful look on his face when he'd pulled her sleeves
back and looked at her shoulders with the pale line of the shirt in a
scoop, but when he looked down now he was not smiling. His
mouth came close and kissed her mouth.

How could that have ever stopped? How could his arms have gone? He nuzzled her neck, he was insistent at her shirt sending thrills through her and she laughed. Do you always behave this way with strangers? she said.

You are not a stranger, he said. Isn't there some place we can go?

# 6. The Sail Closet

H er husband helped her up from the sand in the dark with the waves crashing behind. Before they rejoined the party she pulled her disheveled hair back into a clip. Once inside the light of the open room he walked away from her and plopped down on the couch beside a woman smoking a thin cigar, Dan Shepley's new wife. Ann Lord leaned on an inside windowsill and listened to men discuss money, her heart still beating high and light near the surface of her chest. She shook out her skirt and sand spilled from the hem. Later she caught Oscar's eye across the room, he looked triumphant. On the way home in the car he said, I like how you get around the ocean.

On the knotty dark path moonlight made a lacy pattern on the ground and tree trunks.

Are you leading me into hell? he said.

The trees moved back and they were near the water lapping under the float with an occasional gurgling sound. Silhouetted against the water was the outline of a shed. Ann Grant tugged open the door.

Everything was white. She was picnicking on top of a huge white rock with Glenda the Good Witch. A pale valley spread below with lakes of milk and jagged shores. Suddenly the earth shifted and a great crack zigzagged across the rock which turned out to be papier-mâché. A mist swirled white, there was the nurse's white uniform, her white bedspread, the white tin table on wheels with white cotton balls and white boxes of needles and Oscar's white hats and Oscar's closely cropped white hair.

He was wearing a white hat when she met him in the stands in Saratoga, he had another woman on his arm with a flower in her chignon. We've met before, he said, with a slight accent. He'd grown up in Europe. She did not remember him or the night, still being married to Ted, and now so recently a widow, did not take his flirtations seriously. The long-faced woman gazed off, but Oscar Lord was not discouraged and once again Ann was saved from being too long a time on her own.

He was nearly twenty years older, not tall with a wide chest and round head. He stepped softly in soft leather shoes, wore tailored shirts, was eager-faced with a pensive mouth, unlike himself, made her laugh, breathed quietly in his sleep and after nearly fifteen years of marriage still knocked politely on the bathroom door. He called her Darling, did not remember his dreams, slept in the other room when she was reading, then moved into the other room altogether, was proud of his wife's taste, proud of his daughter Nina, proud like a child of the shape of his feet.

Oscar Lord took her to Rome, he took her to Venice, he could not have children then Virginia happened and the end of the world happened and Ann was pregnant. It was thrilling. Oscar hovered around the baby, the feedings and the changings, nervous, mystified, and when Nina started to walk he'd hold her little hand, take her on excursions he called them, doting on her, so Nina grew up in his glow. He seemed never to age, his skin stayed smooth, only the eyes softened, he liked his wine and his sauces, he put on weight, complained of indigestion, and that Sunday morning in May after breakfast on the porch while the plates were being cleared turned perplexed to the side porch, stretched out on the chaise lounge and fell asleep and did not wake up. He was seventy-four. What had gone on in Oscar's mind Ann did not know. He liked a woman in a great hat, dinner parties, opera. He said it was important to be obstinate but was not in the least. He was in his own world where he smiled frequently to himself and did not wonder overly about his feelings or about his wife or about the feelings his wife had for him. Oscar did not trouble her and by then in her life that was frankly what she preferred.

It might be a good distraction for her, Nina said.

It's a little creepy, Margie said.

She never liked them before, Constance said. She had a little pile of mail in her lap and was opening get well cards. Why should she now?

The circumstances are different.

Yes, said Constance. Worse.

The girls would like it, Teddy said. They love birthday parties.

Then by all means, Constance said. Let's do it for the girls. She wasn't reading the cards, just taking them out of the envelopes and making a pile.

Connie, Margie said. He doesn't mean it that way.

I just think we should think of her first. Am I crazy?

Maybe she would like it, Teddy said quietly. He'd learned long ago that in these matters his sisters would decide without considering his opinion.

Maybe? She can't even blow out one candle much less sixty-five. I think it's a terrible idea.

As if we'd have sixty-five candles, Margie said.

Nina stood over Constance's shoulder and watched what she was doing. We can still celebrate it, she said. Let's have a cake and eat it.

Your philosophy of life, Margie said fondly.

Why not? A card in Constance's hand caught her eye. Who the hell is Peach Howe?

She used to live across the street, Teddy said.

That's right, Constance said, and looked at her brother with surprise.

What? he said. I'm not that out of it.

So what's going to happen to the house? said Nina, moving around. She'd arrived that afternoon and had yet to be affected by the heavy air emanating from the room upstairs.

Jesus, Nina. She's not gone yet, Margie said. Margie lived nearby in an apartment in Central Square but still came home to do laundry. Since June she'd been living full time on Emerson Street back in her old room, next to the guest room where Constance was staying. Nina's room was on the third floor with its own phone line but she had an apartment in New York now. Teddy lived twenty minutes away in Weston with his wife Lauren and twin daughters where he had a contracting business. His partner was picking up the slack while he spent time at his mother's.

She tried to talk to us about the will, Constance said. But no one could really handle it.

Speak for yourself, Teddy said.

We could handle it, Margie said. It was just weird.

Nina brushed her hand over some things in the room, going by the mantelpiece. The only thing I want is the volcano painting, she said, and pointed out toward the hall.

Which happens to be the most valuable thing in the house, Constance said.

It was Daddy's, Nina said.

She's still breathing up there, you guys, Jesus, Margie said.

We're just being practical, Constance said with no conviction whatsoever.

Teddy's wife Lauren brought in a tray with glasses of iced tea with mint sprigs from the garden. She was wearing a stretchy flowered dress with flounces at the knee.

You look pretty today, Teddy said when she sat down beside him.

Thanks, she said. I feel totally fat in this dress.

We should probably sell it, Constance said. And divide it up.

It could generate its own income if you rented it, Lauren said. I was once a real estate agent, you know.

No one responded.

If one of us lived here it'd be a place we could all come to, Margie said. Maybe Teddy wants to live here.

This house, he began. It's not, you know . . . the best things didn't happen here.

No, Margie said.

It's a great house, Nina said. But who wants to live in Cambridge?

Margie looked at her.

Sorry. I mean I wouldn't want to. A thought occurred to her. Why don't you live here? She looked at everyone. Margie should live here.

Oh I couldn't, Margie stuttered sitting up and looking pleased. It's way too big . . . Her eyes were bright. Then she saw the way Nina's mouth was slightly open and saw she wasn't serious and blushed and when neither Constance nor Teddy commented she felt her blush turn prickly. Right, she said, and smiled as if she'd been joking all along.

And in this way nothing was settled.


They lay entwined on unraveling sail bags. Ann Grant had managed to keep her clothes on but they were all shifted around. Her mouth felt overripe. Squares of moonlight showed up on the floor of the shed and on Harris Arden's face. She leaned up on an elbow and looked at him lying with his eyes closed breathing in a controlled way. He took her hand and led it to his hips and pressed it on his pants. He held her arm so she wouldn't take it away and moved her palm over him and when he relaxed his hand she kept moving hers the way he'd shown her. A groan came from the back of his throat, his hand fumbled at her shirt to pull it aside, trying to touch her breasts. She watched his face with its eyes closed and kept moving her hand on him and his head pressed harder against the sail bag. He reached between her legs and her elbow firmly pushed his arm away and his hand strayed back to her shirt and with a jerk pulled it down. He touched her skin slowly and quietly as if the slowness assisted his sense of touch, then his eye opened a sliver to see what he was touching and she saw a gleam in his eye nearly cruel which thrilled her. He closed his eyes and his breath began to come shorter and deeper and he pressed his head back. God his face was beautiful like that. She kept moving her hand and his breath deepened and she watched her hand moving in the shadow then glanced back at his face with the head pressing back staying still. She saw him sort of wince and his mouth open and she heard something catch in the back of his throat which he held sort of ticking there for a long moment then he let air out trailing off nearly whimpering. His face broke into pieces as if in pain then gently relaxed to being placid again but more so. His eyes opened. He looked past her then toward her through her then he saw her and his arms came up surrounding her in a sudden surge as if he were gathering a spinnaker in a high wind pulling her in and pressing her face to his chest. He pulled her in tight.

After a while he relaxed his grip but still held on and kept her close. He murmured in her ear as if reciting a prayer, low and run together, YoualrightyouO.K.?youfeelO.K.?

I'm fine, she said.

That was so—

She lay against his chest. The thought did not come to her and there was no decision to ask, the question simply came out unconsidered and of its own accord. You don't have a girlfriend or anything do you? she said.

Actually, he said right away in a tender voice indicating that this couldn't possibly matter to them, I do.

She stiffened in his arms. You do.

I thought you knew that.

How would I know that?

From Carl. I thought Carl might have told you

I didn't ask Carl. Her voice was suddenly very small.

The air in the sail closet changed.

Ann Grant's eyes were no longer dreamy, they were alert. Her arms became aware of the distinction of his body separate from hers. His body took on its own dimensions, lying alongside her now ominous and strange.

After a while he said, Are you O.K.?

No.

Harris Arden was quiet.

She said, Where is she?

In Chicago.

Ann moved her hand off Harris Arden's arm and though she still leaned against him she no longer clinged on.

She's . . . He cleared his throat. Actually she's coming tomorrow.

Here?

She's taking a seaplane with some people called the Tobins.

Their cousins, Ann whispered.

They're coming first from Boston—

Ann Grant sat forward.

Don't go away, he said.

She did not move further away but did not lean back either. The little shed was no longer sanctuary-like. Its walls seemed to dissolve and she was drawn out to the little grass outside and the sharp rocks below and the water stretching to nowhere.

What's her name? Ann's voice was dull but her mind was lively *this isn't all this couldn't be all there is something else I don't know there's something more to know maybe it will be worse but it will be more it will shift this it will lift me up from this low place I have suddenly been plunged into I cannot suddenly be so low when just moments ago I was so high up.*

Maria, he said.

Maria, said Ann Grant.

I've known her a long time. She waited for me while I was in Korea—

Maria what?

Di Corcia.

How long?

Six years.

Maria, Ann said.

They were silent for a while.

Are you going to marry her?

Again he did not pause but answered matter-of-factly. We're supposed to get married in September.

Ann felt a dull blow hit between her legs. She turned to face him square on. She's your fiancée, she accused.

It was as if an explosion had gone off and now smoke rolled from it filling the air.

Yes, he said.

She could hardly see him anymore in the swirling smoke. It swirled around isolating her. So what are you doing here if you have a fiancée in Chicago?

His answer came right away. Falling in love, he said.

A great wind blasted up clearing the smoke and she saw her feet beneath her standing at the edge of a cliff. So that was it, that was the other part. It came to her in this little shed. So this is what night is for, she thought, this is what arms are for. This is why that window is there, why people sleep at night, why they lie beside each other, what life is. This was the point. She split out of the world with him and everything around them became something sealing off the two of them with no time in it and no endings and no loss or worry. She was full. She set herself back against him very slowly and was silent for a while then turned and touched his face like an explorer with an archeological find and kissed him and lay back again. The great thing was happening to her. She looked up and saw the white painted rafters showing up in the darkness and smelled the wet rope in the corners and saw the pointed flags hanging against the windows in the pitched roof. Her mind spread evenly over everything. *Falling falling* nothing had ever sounded like that *falling in love.*

Every defense she'd ever consciously or unconsciously taken refuge behind suddenly dropped like the buildings you saw demolished in clouds of dust and in its place a new scaffolding was thrown up, a structure upon which she could build a life. His arm was integral to this structure and with its support she felt wide and strong. There seemed to be no difference between herself outside and in. Up until then her personality had been a thing fluctuating in and out of sight like grass underwater and now it was all equally in focus. She was solid, whole. She saw through the window a spiky branch black as antlers in the moonlight.

Look, she said.

He looked. Do you love trees too?

He pulled her near, staying quiet as he did it. He did not know what he did or how everything was changed.


She had no task in front of her, no living room to redo or tickets to pick up, no dinner party to plan, no children to be fetched or novel to be read or phone to be answered, no blue suit to try on when she got home. She stared upward and the ceiling stared back. Stick with the concrete, she told herself. It helped ward off the pain. She tried to think of concrete things. Where she'd lived. Let's see. In New York the first apartment with Phil with the hissing radiators, then the bigger one off Park and Seventy-seventh where Margie was born and they put her in the bottom drawer, then the farmhouse they took for the weekends which Phil never came to, then after the divorce the Rolands' carriage house with iron bannisters. Ted's brick house she never liked, then the house in Connecticut he let her redo and the tangled greenhouse she restored and how the light came in the dusty windows. The rentals. In Easthampton with a black pool. The driftwood one with the dune grass brushing the deck. Paul was carrying a bucket of crabs from the marsh pond. The yellow saltbox on Three O'Clock Island with the lighthouse.

The narrow townhouse she and Oscar took in London, the mill in Provence with the well in the courtyard, the château they shared with the Cutlers with rows of lavender, the villa with the Rolands with the aviary frescoes in the dining room, the mist in Florence, a fireplace going at Christmas, whitewashed walls in Patmos with the pots of rosemary by the blue steps . . . there were little pots of rosemary downstairs on the porch, and bushes of hydrangea and an ancient rhododendron . . . on Gray Gable Road she'd had a tulip magnolia tree blooming cream and pink, and dark eaves and terra cotta tiles in the hall, coming home from school in brown and green shoes, her room had a cranked window with lead panes and ruffles on the bed, a ledge with a china couple dancing a waltz, a brown and yellow radio she listened to doing her math, singing out the window, looking in the mirror, singing on the stage at school . . . what was that? Bees buzzing, or was it a cocktail party on the other side of the fence? She lay under the covers like a clothespin with the bed all around her.

I live in a house of my own, she thought. All I want is someone here beside.

❊   ❊   ❊

I'm thinking of the sail closet, she said.
    Yes.
    You remember that?
    Of course I remember.
    It was nice, she said. Then bad then nice again.
    I remember it as nice.
    I'd never done that so soon with someone.
    I hadn't—well not like that.
    Not with me you mean.
    No. Not like that.
    You said sometimes it was better not doing everything.
    Did I? I must have thought so—for a minute.
    I felt like I'd been punched in the stomach when you told me.

About—?

Her.

I thought you knew.

Then after you said . . . how you felt. I actually thought . . . I thought she didn't matter. It was the surprise of my life.

It was complicated, he said.

I believed other things mattered more.

Love you mean.

That's what I believed then.

And you don't believe it now?

She looked as if she was about to speak but decided against it, not being able to weigh in on either side.

✿  ✿  ✿

She kept taking trains. The windows were so wide she nearly fell out rounding the corners. The twins got off at one stop to buy tiger Popsicles but didn't get back on and the train started without them. She sat with her father who drank from a silver flask. It was his medicine, medicine was not for little girls. They passed a snowy field with crows. A hobo walked down the aisle carrying a globe on the end of a stick. He lifted her skirt with the end of his stick, peering between her legs. I bring you the world, he said.

Then she was on a train going to Washington, D.C., to visit Ted's mother. In the seat facing her was a little girl traveling with her father. He was clearly fond of her but had difficulty removing her sweater and didn't notice an untied shoelace dangling as the train chugged along. Ann Stackpole leaned forward and tied it. She lifted the little girl's hair out of the collar of her sweater and the little girl looked back at her with such a greedy look Ann Stackpole wondered if she had a mother. The father fumbled through a bag, glancing at Ann now and then apologetically. He took out a pad of paper and some crayons and poured them into the little girl's lap hoping she'd know what to do. The little girl began to draw, fingers clenched white, oblivious of the train's agitation. She was drawing an animal. It looked very much like the diamond leopard pin Ann had pinned to her lapel, a birthday present from Ted. The little girl caught Ann looking, flashing up light-colored eyes at her. Ann Stackpole had by then four children of her own so her reaction was odd. It was as if she'd been pushed into a bright room, had the door slammed and was locked in. Seeing the girl's light-colored eyes struck her and she thought, This is the child I would have had with him. This was our little girl.


What's going to happen now? she said.

Something has already happened, hasn't it? he said. His arm tightened around her as they walked back in the darkness of the wet garden.

It has. She did not look at him.

This may be the end of something for me. He sounded distressed. The end of a long thing.

Her heart was rejoicing but she hid it, out of respect. Do things end so easily? She even felt sympathetic toward the unknown girl.

Not easily.

How long have you known her?

I don't know if I want to talk about this.

She let go of his waist. I was just wondering.

He took her hand. She's a good person. She loves me.

Ann had noticed how a woman's love often inspired a sense of duty in men.

Do you love her?

I do, he said. Ann's chest cramped. But, it's different.

Later she would learn it was always different, with each person of course it was different. But at the time this consoled her.

Where did you meet her?

Do you want to know this really?

I do. His hand was in hers as they walked up the hill.

I met her six years ago downtown on a tramcar.

Really? A stranger?

She was a girl sitting in a blue coat.

And what did you do?

I went up and started talking to her.

Do you do that a lot?

I'd never done it before. I didn't think about it. I thought she was beautiful.

Then what?

I asked her for her number.

Did she give it to you?

No. But she gave me an address and said I could write her if I wanted. She said it as if she didn't think I would.

Did you?

I delivered the letter myself. She lived on the North Shore.

You showed up. That was bold of you.

She said she had hoped I would. Then we fell in love. I think I fell in love first.

Then . . . Ann began, but thought better of it and shook her head.

Harris Arden grew thoughtful. She's a good person, he said.

Ann did not care to hear this a third time. When does she get here?

Tomorrow afternoon, he said, and looked up at the sky. Today.


The sheets were stacked on a shelf. The first sheet she pulled out was blue which meant it was time to prepare herself for a ceremony. Next came a flat yellow sheet. The yellow sheets were to be used as envelopes and she would have to address them. Someone had stuffed back a grey sheet which she pulled out crumpled and un-ironed. This stood for the afternoon. Last came a pink sheet with a scalloped border. The pink sheet was the last sheet she'd use.

She felt someone in the room.

Who is it? she said.

It's Margie, Mother. And Teddy, said the same voice. Teddy's here.

And Constance, Mother. I'm here too.

And me. It was Nina's voice.

And Nurse Brown, said Margie. She's here. We're all here.

Ann Lord opened her eyes. Her children stood before her, pillars not holding anything up. Yes . . . she said. Everyone's here but me.

# 7. A PALE BAY

She kept the curtains back in the day and in the night. Her parents had slept with the shades down and on the rare occasion Ann dared enter their room it was always pitch black or in the morning with slivers of light outlining the windows. Her mother wore a sleeping mask over her face cream, and earplugs. Ann's father snored. Her mother blocked out a lot to achieve peace.

Mrs. Grant worked as a seamstress at the good shops on Newbury Street, fitting the society ladies whose names appeared in the gossip columns. The facts, Mrs. Grant knew, were always a little off. Henrietta Bradley was not in the least interested in Stitch Poor, she had her eye on Dick Drummond, and they had Louise Drinkwater splendid in violet tulle which Mrs. Grant knew having put the dress on Louise herself was blue. The Homans sisters devoted? Those two couldn't stand each other. Never believe what you read, Ann, she told her daughter, squinting as she threaded a needle, And never believe what other people say.

But Ann had heard from her Aunt Joy about an old beau of her mother's. According to Aunt Joy she'd been in love with Randall Pingree, a boy from a good family in Boston. Ellen Kearney had met him on account of their mother being a schoolteacher so the Kearney sisters, Ellen and Joy, could attend private school. The way Aunt Joy told it Randall Pingree had been in love with Ann's mother and it didn't occur to her not to give everything to him. This had, Aunt Joy said, affected her reputation. At first it was very romantic till it became clear that the boy couldn't possibly marry Ellen Kearney and when this became apparent to Ellen herself it was as if someone had told her she was walking on ground when all the time she had believed she was swimming in water. Aunt Joy said it changed her. She had been carrying her feeling up high like a flag flapping and meeting this barrier to her happiness she put down her flag in protest and lay it unflapping on the ground and continued forward into the battle of life with her feelings, those foolish things, no longer in the forefront. This was how Aunt Joy put it. She let herself be guided by other things, pursued her interest in clothes, apprenticed with a French tailor, no longer at the mercy of disappointment. She took satisfaction in her work and in knowing about the lives of the society ladies, who were living the life she might have had if things had been otherwise.

Ann's father was an assistant foreman in a leather factory. Before dinner if her father wasn't home Ann would walk on the shady side of Gray Gable Road with the evening light on the other side and turn onto Mass. Ave. where the street was wider with no trees to the middle of the block. In the summer with the doors open she could smell Patsy's from down the street. Walking into the darkness she first saw reddish lights then the dark shapes with the bottles behind and a green glass lamp and her father's syrupy voice saying, Here's my angel of mercy come to fetch me. He bent down but his eyes couldn't aim very well and his gaze sort of tumbled by. He got up off his stool. So long Ed, said the man next to him, and the man behind the counter said, Mr. Grant, as his palm came forward onto the bills left crumpled. Sometimes Ann carried his heavy coat and they walked up the hill around the cracked ice past Mrs. Shulte in her window and sometimes saw the orange cat her father called Butterscotch Pudding though they didn't know its real name or whose it was. His hand pressed down on her shoulder and she stayed still to keep steady.

What did you do today, angel? he said.

Just school.

And how was school?

Danny Block got an icicle in his eye and went to the hospital.

Did he? Good, good. Her father was always smiling after he'd been at Patsy's.

Ann's mother's face was tight putting the napkins around the dining room table which was on one side of the living room.

Smells grand, said her father as Ann steered him to his chair, trying to disturb as few pieces of furniture as possible. He sat down then got up immediately and picked his way out of the room as if leaning into a gale. When he returned he held onto the door frame surprised how solid it was and trying to hide his surprise. His hair was slicked back with water and his face more alert but the gaze still wandered. He took his seat.

Ann's mother never once said anything about her father's behavior. She turned her opinions to other matters. She served the food and as the three of them began to eat Mrs. Grant's stiff face relaxed and she talked. The current of her talk floated them through dinner. Ann did not always understand her innuendos—and did not ask. It gave Mrs. Grant a sort of dim glow to talk about what was happening in the neighborhood, what parties her clients had attended, who came into the shop that day. She got a faraway look harkening back to her days at parties and hinted at beaux and her desirability before she'd met Edgar Grant but strangely never mentioned Randall Pingree. She told Ann to sit up straight. They used to dance till all hours. She'd found some good lampshades at Mamie Sturges', Ed had a piece of potato on his chin, they were a little expensive but something of good quality lasted and it was worth it for pretty things. Ed Grant nodded along with the hum of her voice, he looked up at her, grateful that everything was being looked after and he went back to eating his stew.

The smell of bacon, the kitchen door. Ann Grant was nearly knocked over by a golden retriever as she opened the screen. Can Wallis come in? she said as the dog shot through the kitchen and disappeared inside.

The Wittenborns' dining room was large with a sideboard and built-in shelves with blue and white Canton china, but at breakfast time they ate in the kitchen, crowding around the beaten linoleum table. Off the kitchen was a honeycomb of various pantries and larders and clutter closets growing smaller and darker as they went off to the end of the house. In a narrow closet the size of a coffin Mrs. Wittenborn in a crisp piqué tennis dress held a telephone to her ear. Uh-huh, she said. Uh-huh, uh-huh. Right. Uh-huh uh-huh-uh-huh . . . She rubbed her cheek nodding. Mmm-hmmm, mmm-hmmm.

Ann tried to look at everyone equally for Harris Arden was there among them, leaning against the counter with his ankles crossed, holding a cup of coffee. She compared this to the idea of him which occupied her before falling asleep and found him even better in the flesh with his legs longer and his arms it seemed bigger. She caught his eye for the smallest fraction of a second, reaching for a glass of orange juice and knocking it over. Lizzie Tull was there with a sponge, in her tennis whites, already having gotten in a couple of sets that morning.

There's no wind but we should go anyway, Buddy was saying. He wore pajamas with red piping and a flyer's cap with the flaps over his ears.

Handsome slippers, Ann said.

Christmas from Lila, he said, and tried to keep back a smile.

Gigi banged on the door, her arms full of bay branches. She was framed in the screen with bits of leaf stuck in her hair.

You look like a painting, said Harris Arden, opening the door.

So he said that sort of thing to other girls. Of course he would.

Why wouldn't he?

These are for the church, she said, shining at him. Here.

Harris put down his cup and took the branches which turned small in his arms. Gigi reached into an upper cabinet and clattered around.

Ralph Eastman was spooning scrambled eggs onto a plate in front of Ann. Bacon or sausage? he said.

Is that Mrs. Babbage's apron you have on?

I am the only one she lets wear it, Ralph explained.

Carl and Lila came in. The church is like an oven, he said cheerfully. He wore an old sun hat balanced on top of his head.

Lila was wearing a blue and white striped shirt and red lipstick against her white teeth. Around her was an air of peace. She always had a calm aura around her, but it was particularly striking now in the midst of the wedding preparations which were mounting with symphonic tempo.

She sat down near Ann. Where did you disappear to last night? she whispered. Ann smiled, this would be discussed later.

Mrs. Wittenborn came out of the phone closet. Vee and Dee are getting in around five, she said.

Ann was conscious of Harris Arden busy at the sink with Gigi, and did not look over. *Something has already happened hasn't it*

Vernon asked if you were up, Ann. Mrs. Wittenborn raised her eyebrows.

He's still not over Ann, Gigi said over her shoulder.

Ann directed her attention to salting her eggs. She heard branches snapping, the back at the sink did not turn around.

Gigi kept talking. I don't think he'll ever get over you. He's even got another girlfriend. Was Gigi touching him?

Kingie, said Ralph, holding up a spatula.

Kingie? Carl said to Lila.

I told you, Lila said.

Have I met her? said Mrs. Wittenborn.

She was the one in the yellow dress at the Morgans'.

The sort of lace affair? Mrs. Wittenborn shook her head. It wasn't good.

Here, Gigi said to Harris. Hold this?

Ann could not see Harris' face.

Has Ann met her? Ralph said, looking at Ann.

No. I don't really—

Well she'll meet her later. Vernon's bringing her. Mrs. Wittenborn looked for a place to flick her ash. Morning darling.

Morning Linda. Dick Wittenborn brought in the smell of aftershave and a faint whiff of alcohol. Morning all.

Harris Arden turned to join everyone in the greeting. He caught Ann's eye and showed he had not forgotten and the same charge of the night before ran through her again.

Harris' fiancée is coming with them too? said Mrs. Wittenborn.

Harris turned around the other way to her. Yes, he said with a polite open face. Maria.

Ann felt Lila's glance but wasn't prepared to return it.

Maria? Ralph said. He stepped forward, this was new information.

Maria di Corcia.

She from Chi-town too? Buddy said.

Harris nodded.

What does she do? Lila said.

The conversation went on. *Fiancée Harper's Bazaar in the Chicago office wedding in September.* Ann felt as if a heavy boot were on her chest, slowly crushing her lungs.

Her breathing was shallow. The I.V. rose above her like a flagpole festooned with transparent ribbons. A swollen plastic bag dangled from the top and at the end of its tube was a narrow cap over the needle which could be inserted into the plastic valve which had a permanent place in the back of Ann Lord's veined hand.

Her legs and arms were being moved and she watched the sheet fold back then rolled on her side then felt the sheet being pulled under her and rolled back. The nurse tucked it. This was not her body she looked at, the leg with the long bone, the hip jutting out.

She recognized it but it belonged to someone else. My God, it belonged to her mother.

*Let's slip this off, this arm first. That's it.* A warm sponge moved over her shoulders. Strange how little people were naked. *Won't you take off your coat can I take that for you here let me thank you not at all would you mind if I undid this what are you doing just one button I can't reach the hook would you mind I can't seem to manage what would you do without me here let me take this off I like to undo it may I will you let me I want to see you I think I better leave this on.* There was a black sky and black lawn and the dwindling of a car motor. She stood high up at a sealed window with sheets behind her twisted on the floor and the sky pink and water towers like bullets dotting the rooftops. She stood at tall French doors in bright noon light with a shower running behind and when she opened the latch the loud revving of *motorinos* and cars going round and round, the black and white statue of horses and pointed wings, the balcony shallow in this foreign place thinking what to put on and wear and standing naked at the window thinking this might be the nearest thing to showing herself truly.

Someone was sobbing down the hall in one of the guest rooms then it turned into waves. The sea, she thought, the sea, she'd not seen the sea in the longest time. God she'd love to swim.

She shot herself out of a cannon and flew from the house. The lawn below grew small and the rooftops of the Cambridge houses turned flat and square. She followed the grey snake of the Charles River up to the Tobin Bridge then swung inland at Saugus up Route One's strip of giant liquor stores and candy kitchens and Chinese restaurants off toward the green summer hills of New Hampshire passing into Maine and the ridge of captain's houses above Portland onto the two lane road winding by shimmering marshes and fields of Queen Anne's lace and farmhouses and cornfields and pear orchards over Wiscasset and Waldoboro and Thomaston past the cement factory with its brown grass onto the

Main Street of Rockland built of brick down to the ferry landing and its fat pilings over the fish factory into the harbor soaring over the narrow stone breakwater nearly a mile long with the lighthouse at the end past Owls Head across from it blinking into the bay by the gong and the stone monument and into the channel with the smaller islands and cormorants drying their wings over the pole-held floats squeaking into the center of town and the slanting lawn with its curving picket fence and the elm tree shadows out past the school's dusty swings over the fork in the road dipping by the rushes by the shining mudflats with the islands way off in a hundred dark humps past the white cube of the Grange Hall around to the Bishops Harbor bridge and the flat water of the inner harbor up over the cedars to the house on the bluff where the tent tilted in the field and the long porch flanked the house and below a path cut through high grass to the rock garden then the stone steps down to the dock above the curved flint-scattered beach where in the morning the water was still and green waiting

The dull thud of stakes being hammered echoed in the still air.

They stood beneath a limp flag. The world was as still as if there were no air and the sky was bleached out and the water like spilled paint. At the end of the Wittenborns' dock a schooner was being busily cranked at and unfurled while people stood waiting holding bags and towels and baskets. They arrived in sunglasses. Gail Slater wore a man's shirt over her bathing suit, Carl's quiet friend Monty had a nose of white zinc, Mrs. Wittenborn's straw hat cast a checkerboard across her face. What had they said? Was Lizzie Tull talking about the seating for the bridal dinner, or Ralph checking to make sure the sandwiches were in the plaid bag? Ann could not remember. But she remembered Harris Arden stepping under the boom then stepping over the railing and holding down the cord so they could come aboard. His hair was a fine cloud in the bright air. And after they were under sail she remembered sitting beside him in the center of the boat in the shade while he showed her how a heartbeat has two beats inside one, *tha-thump tha-thump,* and the sleepy feeling she had as his fingers thumped her arm.

The wind did not pick up. The surface of the bay stayed soft as poured glass. They motored out from shore then turned off the engine and drifted. She sat near him in the bright shade of the mainsail and they didn't talk about who was arriving later on the plane. There was no point in talking about that though Ann Grant had grown more curious about what this Maria di Corcia looked like and what else had gone on between them and how it was different. Harris Arden told her about his family, he was the youngest, his father was nearly eighty. The brother had pretty much gone off into shady business practices. His sisters were both married with children. She saw his family as if it were steps up to a monument. The monument was not something she had.

Up at the bow Gigi lay with her cheek pressed to the studs on the gunwale staring at the molten water moving slowly by. Her legs were stretched out behind her slightly apart. There was no wind, no air, no breath. Ann sat beside Harris Arden. She did not need to touch him, she didn't need anything as long as he stayed near. The men had taken off their shirts and his arms were bare against the milky sea.


There was a terrible racket, the halyards clanging, the canvas snapping. Something flipped in her head and the sea was navy blue and blown into white tips and the sails heading into the wind were careening. The Coast Guard captain was holding onto the side of the boat bobbing up and down and Ann brushed the hair from her eyes and saw Oscar's face turning and the look of pity and fear.


There was no wind, it was still. The schooner sat on top of the bay. The boom glided from side to side and people were dragging behind in an inner tube further slowing the boat's progress and he walked up the deck carrying a plate into the shade beside her and held out the plate as if they'd known each other a long time and didn't need to speak and she took a sandwich triangle with the crust cut off and they watched the water go by.

Carl stood at the stern with his hand on the huge wheel, people in the cockpit chatted softly over Bloody Marys, their words inaudible. A herring gull cawed. In the distance a motorboat buzzed by and they could hear people talking beneath the sound of the motor then it was quiet again.

There was a splash. Ann turned to a space beside her. She looked in the water. He was swimming alongside the slow boat.

Aren't you coming in? he said as if it were something they'd discussed.

She stood up, took off her sunglasses, snapped down the back of her bathing suit and dove in. The cold water was a shock, and colder down at her feet. But she was used to long swims. Past the breakers in Cohasset where the water was warmer she'd turn around to find the shore quickly far off and the houses small and the dune grass a feathery line. She liked the feeling of the swells lifting her up and rolling beneath her. They swam away from the boat. They went faster than the boat. Ann got ahead of him then he swam ahead of her. He said she swam well and she told him she used to be in swimming contests, not caring if it sounded like boasting.

She swam with Harris and thought of how his fiancée was arriving later that day and if she would have a chance to be alone again with him the way they'd been last night. It seemed it ought to be possible, but when she tried to imagine she saw that it was less and less likely. Maria di Corcia knew no one else and would naturally stay by Harris and he being Harris would look after her. He was that sort. Tonight was the bridal dinner at the Yacht Club then the wedding tomorrow and the reception after and then it would be Sunday and they would all leave the island and the whole time he would be with his fiancée. Ann would probably not get a chance to talk to him much more and then back he'd go to Chicago—with her—and he and Maria would . . . what would they do? What would he do? *Stay like that stay like that always something has already happened* She did not want to stop swimming. She would have liked to keep swimming with him out into the bay forever.

They'd all stood at this door. Margie stood hesitating as she'd hesitated at so many other of her mother's doors, waiting for her to be through with her nap, out of the tub, finished getting dressed, or in the middle of the night by some fluke to be still awake and willing to take her back to bed. A vase of cosmos she'd picked from the garden was balanced in one hand, not that they needed any more flowers but these were everywhere like small tangled trees. She unclicked the knob and gently pushed the door.

Her mother was awake and the nurse was bent over her and both their faces turned sharply toward the door.

Give us a minute, said the nurse, her profile melting into the window light behind. Behind her massive white back Margie saw her mother's face unrecognizable with an expression of panic and she immediately backed out. It was an expression she'd never seen before and with the air of secrecy and preparation and the peculiar fused position of her mother's body with the nurse Margie felt she'd walked in on some forbidden rite.

She stood in the hall with her heart beating in a sped-up unnatural way. She put the vase down on the floor off the rug and turned down the stairs. In the library she heard Constance on the phone speaking French. At the end of the hall she saw Teddy's wife Lauren in the kitchen with Mrs. Kelley and Pat Vincent, each holding one of the twins on their laps. Margie snapped up her pouch with the satin cord on the hall table and knocked open the wide screen door taking the porch steps quickly, her tennis shoes flapping against her heels.

She took the gravel path through the granite posts between the hedge out to Emerson Street. She went in the direction of the Square. It was nearly seven and the streets were quiet and the lawns off the sidewalk humped in deep shade. She hurried across the street, half-seeing the car which braked and honked, and didn't look back. Her sneaker slipped off and she reached back impatient to hook it around her heel, not stopping, nearly tripping, catching herself in time. She turned at the end of the street. She was about to burst.

Around the corner. Finally out of sight of the house, finally away from the tall shutters along the porch and the lantern above the door and the black shingled roof and the upper windows watching after her. A pocket of air rose in her lungs, or a bubble of non-air, making it hard to breathe and she walked swiftly. Up ahead loomed the figures of two men walking a dog, she couldn't face anyone, she turned onto a street she never took.

The pressure kept expanding inside her. The sidewalk erupted in cracks and roots and above her branches frayed and she felt that if anyone stepped out of their door the force whirling around her would blast them back in or hurl them down like a sack of rags.

Her mother's face came back to her past the large arm of the nurse with an expression which seemed to say, Go away, you're going to take away my comfort, go away! and the bulging knot in Margie's chest popped and no sound came from her mouth as her body was wracked with sobs on this unknown street. She tried to stay ahead of the waves sweeping up from inside her. It was not unlike the surge she'd felt with Seth in Bali when she'd been so sick overboard. He'd held her forehead with a cool hand firmly not in the least put off and muttered soothing words. Now the sobs came longer remembering how she'd not been seasick after all. Then they decided they weren't ready to have a baby, that is Seth wasn't ready, not yet, they would, eventually they would, they were married weren't they, but just not yet. So she'd gotten rid of it and had lost that. Then she'd lost Seth and now there was her mother . . . eventually one lost everything. She flushed with shame to feel sorry for herself while her mother lay there with so much more to feel sorry about and the sobs surged afresh.

After a while her crying softened. She began to catch her breath. A tingling rose in her temples, she felt her cheeks hot. She stopped, shaken and worn out. The reason they never walked on this street

was that it ended in someone's driveway. She looked around. In the
houses were people with many lives she would never know. It was a
summer evening in late July. People were getting home from work
or already were home. Maybe they were having drinks, feeding
babies. Maybe someone read a book, lit a pipe, walked down stairs.
None of them was her mother. She heard a window shudder.
Through the tangle of trees the sun was setting and the small
orange diamond of it flashed, hitting Margie in the eye.

She retraced her steps back down the street they never took.
The two men with the dog were gone. She followed the curving
brick sidewalk, crossed the wider street with traffic going both
ways, and took Radcliffe Way past the half-stone house with the
television going inside, over the sidewalk stained wet from a sprin-
kler. She put her sunglasses on before reaching Brattle Street, feeling blank and drugged and numb. Back at the house was pain that
did not stop, that would keep going, having no purpose, adding up
to nothing, continuing until it ended. She stepped up to the market on the corner.

She took out of her basket and put on the counter a yellow
bottle of Joy, three green apples, a bulb of garlic, a blue box
of spaghetti, mushrooms under plastic in a purple container, an
orange packet of batteries. The Asian woman at the cash register
sometimes seemed to know her and sometimes didn't. This time
she seemed to and smiled. Margie asked for paper not plastic and
put the items in the bag herself. She waited at the door while an
old man who was coming in took the steps very slowly tapping his
foot forward. Her mother would never be that old.

The evening light flooded Brattle Street which for a moment
had no cars on it and the surface shone gold.

At home the flowers had been taken off the hall floor. In her
mother's room sat Mrs. Kelley and Pat Vincent. Margie tilted in
the door as Mrs. Kelley was saying she'd just gotten a postcard
from her son who was driving his family across the country, they'd
stopped in New Mexico to see Buddy Cutler who as they knew had
married the part-Indian girl who according to her son couldn't be
nicer though maybe not the brightest girl and they had four kids

and Buddy seemed to be doing very well with his business selling cactus plants. They were all having a super time.

Her mother's eyelids were heavy from the drugs. She pointed to the cosmos. Where did those come from? she said in her new slow voice.

Margie said she'd picked them from the garden.

Tell her I love her, said Ann Lord, and she closed her eyes.


I don't know how you can last in there, said Ralph Eastman when Ann Grant and Harris Arden climbed up the schooner ladder. Aren't you freezing?

Harris handed her a towel. It was the only towel around and it occurred to Ann how Malcolm Flynn would have passed her the towel after quickly drying himself off first and even Vernon Tobin would have wiped his face before passing it on. Harris Arden gave her the towel while he dripped.

They sat in the sun to warm up. The engine kicked on and a sigh of protest rose up from the ship.

We'll never get back in time otherwise, Ralph said.

Let's never *go* back, Buddy said. He had a wet towel wrapped turban-style around his head. Gail Slater sat beside him with her long arms and long legs folded up like origami and Ann noticed a familiar worshipful look when her face tilted in Buddy's direction. Ann had seen the look again and again on girls near Buddy. He liked quiet girls. Sometimes one never heard a word out of Buddy's girls. They slumped in a posture of admiration, hypnotized. He seemed to cast a spell over them with no effort whatsoever. One summer he'd even turned his idle attention to Ann. There was one afternoon they'd ridden bikes to an abandoned farmhouse, stolen plums, and lay eating them under a tree. He'd taken a splinter out of her hand, and Ann had started to see him in a different way. Then he'd gotten distracted by the buxom Preston sisters. Ann had minded at the time but soon grew proud of having escaped being one of those girls swooning over Buddy Wittenborn.

The water was satin. Harris' hand came toward her and she thought crazily he was going to grab her and pull her over. Instead he removed a thin green ribbon of seaweed stuck to her shoulder. Up at the bow Gigi lay unmoving in the same position as if nailed to the deck.


Don't turn on the engine, she said.

We won't.

It's coming in from the south, said Ann Lord.

Teddy and Margie exchanged glances. Their mother looked through them.

A person is like a porpoise, she said solemnly.

Teddy and Margie started to laugh and left the room, pushing each other, not wanting to embarrass her.


But they did, they did turn on the engine and they kept it on. The hum took over the silence and the boat which had been drifting unsteerable into the glassy bay now pointed unwavering with a slicing bow back toward the bristled silhouette of Three O'Clock Island. The water passed in striped ripples beneath their feet dangling over the side. Gulls flew by weaving around each other and Ann Grant felt there was a purpose behind everything which she understood but could not put into words. Maybe music could explain it, words were too flat.

The man beside her was a tree.

At the stern Lila and Carl sat with their backs to the boat. Lila's head rested on Carl's shoulder as he talked to her and she nodded, keeping her head against him.

Gigi Wittenborn materialized on the other side of Harris. Even waking from a nap she seemed to be coming from some adventure. A whole crowd of people seemed to stare out from her lit face.

You were asleep a long time, Harris said. I hope it's not that bump on the head.

I wasn't sleeping, Gigi said. I was dreaming.

They faced out. Not far from the boat the sleek back of a porpoise slid up with its flat fin and rolled forward like the top of a wheel then slipped under again. Ann glanced at Harris Arden. He wasn't wearing sunglasses and his eyes were suffused with light. Everything is in the eyes, she thought. The porpoises—there were two—swam alongside the boat without looking over, quick to attach themselves, unquestioning and proprietary. Ann Grant looked at his mouth with the crease in the bottom lip. Everything is in the mouth, she thought. For a moment the difficulties of their situation pricked her but she quickly assumed they would be resolved.

Look over there, someone said. Coming from the south.

Around the western tip of Perry's Point plowing forward like a huge white snowbank was white mist tumbling with curls of steam dissolving upward in wisps.

It looks like an avalanche, someone said.

Ann looked at the encroaching fog. She felt it was coming for her.

❖   ❖   ❖

Ask me again.

What?

To look at you.

What do you mean?

The way you did.

He was silent for a while. I'm not sure I can go back that far. Can we? It wouldn't be the same.

That's alright, she said. I have it here. She closed her eyes and knocked her fist on her breast.

❖   ❖   ❖

The sheet on her knee rolled into a glassy swell. His hand came toward her again and touched the small of her back where her bathing suit dipped and his palm was cool.

Are you sunburned? he said. His hand on her back seemed to say, This is you. This is who you are under my hand. The boat moving made a breeze but the water's surface remained still. You have a nice back, he said. This was how he would tend a patient, she thought, looking down, thinking what to do next.

You must have seen some awful things in Korea, she said.

He looked at her oddly and took his hand away. I don't think about it, he said. It doesn't help to think about.

She ought not to have brought it up. You must think normal life awfully usual, she said, meaning to apologize.

Not at all. He said nothing for a while then with an effort said, Not at all. It's something which took place on another planet, it has so little to do with what's here. Every once in a while I think . . . he trailed off. There were people there who . . . He shook his head. Anyway, he said, I don't.

I can't imagine it, she said.

One thing I liked about playing music, he said. You don't have to talk about it. You just do it. I like that.


Before sunrise she watched the sky in little pieces between the leaves change from dark blue to pink to white. She'd once had a life but was no longer in it. Nights without sleep and hours spent staring did not make up a life. For moments the pain lifted like a sail filling with wind and the white bed sailed along then something slid under digging in its points and the wheels began to churn and the steel machine to hum. One endured suffering but it never took any shape, it was made simply to be borne. It produced nothing and after it was over was forgotten.

Where to turn? She looked about the room, into the corners, out the windows. She lay and lay and lay and lay. It seemed as if she'd been crossing this ceiling all her life. She wanted a song to sing, she wanted to be singing. Where had her life gone? She'd not even had it. An old longing billowed out like a curtain in a gazebo, flapping out as if to say, there was something you wanted . . . Someone was snapping his fingers in time with the music. Someone was playing

Duke Ellington through the trees. He played beautifully. Will you have dinner with me? he said. He had nervous dark eyebrows, was thin as a wire. He nodded a lot, encouraging himself, and snapped his fingers as if biting off something hard. There was a song on the radio, it was one of his singers, he took her to a low-ceilinged room where a band played hunched over their instruments, they were let in without tickets, smoke filled the wedges of light. He got up to play. He played piano with the boys onstage. The music was lively and filled up the room. He looked stricken smiling after applause, then sang "Imagination" and her knees buckled hearing his voice and she leaned against a column. Other people listened sitting at tables or dancing, some more rapt than others but all were under the spell. The music fell over her like a net and she thought of Phil Katz in a new way. He was a sort of poet. She never thought of him as a husband or a father and actually neither did he and yet that's what he became, for a while.

He brought her soup when she had the flu reading Nancy Mitford and talked nonstop and when he kissed her she said he might get sick and he said, I'm not too concerned.

He held out his hand, he pulled her off the bench, his arm was wiry and firm, he was smiling, she was lost and did not know it. She took his arm. They walked by towering buildings, she looked up, he looked down, it had been raining. She could not remember what she said, she remembered holding onto his arm. They were wed at City Hall. She felt she was herself sometimes then at other times felt she was just another girl. He said my wife, she sat beside him driving into the sun, he called her from the next room, she ironed his shirt, he waited while she got dressed. Then she couldn't fit into any of her clothes.

They had a little girl, Constance. Phil had wanted a girl. Then another, Margie right away. She was scrambling eggs, Phil was slamming the door, she made deviled eggs, Phil wore a hat. They took a picnic in the park wearing sunglasses, they ate half an egg salad sandwich, walked the baby carriage on Monday. Sunday Phil slept all day. He took her out, he came home late, he came home at dawn. He took Constance on his bony knee, Margie was wrapped in an eyelet blanket. Fiona Speed stopped by in a new Chanel suit. Phil hitched his arm into his overcoat hurrying out. Margie lay in the crib, strawberries on her jumper, Constance wore a pom-pom on her hat, Phil's knee beating in time with the music. *Don't get around much anymore . . .*

Her face changed after the babies. At night the music was louder, she left early, Phil put her in a cab and went back to the people he had to see. At home she paid the babysitter, fed Margie. Her sweater smelled of smoke, tears were streaming down her cheeks. Phil had an office in midtown. In at noon, home for dinner, out again. His clients were three singers and one band, a few musicians who came and went. She wrote checks from the family account. Phil had the business account which also went to backing other enterprises, shaky despite inside tips, visits to the racetrack. He stood very still sweating as the horses ran and if he won burst into a sort of spasm, his arms awkward, not like you'd expect from a musician. When he lost he stayed away from the apartment and the flowered chairs and Ann not looking at him. His daughters looked at him with his own brown eyes.

She needed a walk, she needed some air, she took a walk *is there something wrong* when she got back, *Yes I thought, You tell me, I already . . . we already . . . What's the matter leave me alone why do you care what does it matter I just thought it shouldn't matter I will always this is the last time I won't what now not again Phil Phil not again I will always be I just wanted my wife they said I will always they said I just want to make it better I just what were you thinking I thought I could I thought we were I thought I'd be I thought you you were wrong I want to spend it with you I thought you were right I didn't know you were enough you were not enough if only you had if only you could when did this happen it was always it was never so this is the room where we say good-bye no that was somewhere else not them that was before is there some-one else that doesn't have to do with us is there someone* it was too late it was always too late *I should never have I should have known*

*I didn't want I didn't mean I will always I will never who is she nobody no one*

She was no one, she was Gina Harvey one of his singers, cross-eyed with plucked eyebrows, but he'd never been with her on the same day if he'd been with Ann. That was a point of honor with him, he told her after the divorce. And it hadn't been so easy either.

She took off her ring, it went into a box, it was still in the box. She crossed the street in the snow holding the children's hands after signing the papers stepping over the slush in ankle boots and nylons, she packed the clothes and furniture, moved to the country, wore low heels. She slept in a new bed without Phil. He stayed in the city, took the girls to the zoo, then he was going to Paris for a short trip. That was the last she heard. Months later some men not reputable came looking for Phil Katz at the Rolands' carriage house and she could say without having to lie that she'd not the slightest idea what had become of her ex-husband whom her daughters never saw again but she hoped he was well.


She breathed in against the pillow, smelling the balsam. Across the bay the islands were washed in haze. They motored into Bishops Harbor past the rock they called the Pulpit. Pain flooded through her, she was shot back into her small frame, Phil was being dragged out the door, she noticed a curled brown burr in the bouquet of cosmos and wanted to snap it off but her arms were snapped off and lay there unable to lift up. Leaves against the window, that was here. Light dappled on the sill, here too. Glass clicking on the table. Here. The sound of water slapping a dock. Not here.

She was with the water.

They walked up the ramp of green sandpaper, and paused to look toward the bay where the fog bank was now a wall blocking the entrance to the harbor.

No plane's going to get through that, Carl said. No boat either.

Harris stood beside him assessing the situation. Maria hates to fly, he said.

Ann was walking by and having her name spoken to someone else Maria suddenly sprouted up real.

I'm making a complete mess, Margie said, hunched over her toes.

Anyway, Constance said, concentrating on brushing polish on her thumb, the article said that patients let go once they've said good-bye to everyone.

That's ridiculous, Nina said, waving her hands and feet languidly in the air. As if you can choose.

Who else does she have to say good-bye to? Teddy said.

I hate saying good-bye, Margie said.

Who likes it? Nina said. She studied a fingernail to see if it was dry. Everyone's always saying they hate to say good-bye as if they're revealing some rare personality trait. People should say if they *like* to say good-bye. I've never known anyone who did.

I have, Teddy said.

Who?

Me. He stood up. I'm leaving the menstrual hut, he said and left his sisters smiling.

Mrs. Wittenborn and Lila sat at the dining room table, puzzling over the gaps left in the evening's seating plan. Lila took a cigarette from her mother's pack on the table and Mrs. Wittenborn, not looking at her, said, Don't let your father see that. Ann Grant took the traveling skirt of Lila's she'd promised to hem and went onto the back porch. Outside she could still overhear Harris Arden in the telephone closet, only the tone of his voice but it was enough to tell her he was talking to the girl. After sitting for a moment she stood up and walked around to the front porch where through the screen door she saw Gigi standing in the hallway listening either to her mother and sister arguing or to Harris' conversation. Ann took her needle and thread onto the lawn. Pacing down near the pink mallow was Ralph Eastman holding a piece of paper, gesturing with his hands, practicing his toast. She turned back to the guest cottage and as she approached the open windows heard the voices of Lizzie Tull and Gail Slater inside as they tied ribbons around the bridesmaids' bouquets mentioning Ann's name in conjunction with Harris Arden. Ann turned around. She took the path down to the rock garden. When she came out of the trees she found the small round lawn occupied by Buddy Wittenborn lying asleep on his back with his bare feet crossed and his hands folded on his chest in protection and then she saw he wasn't asleep though his glasses with the black topped frames were set up on his forehead. His eyes were open and he was gazing up.

How is she today?

I can hear you, Grace. I'm awake.

Ann, how are you? No, Fergus, over here.

What are they doing down there? said Ann Lord.

Painting their nails. Grace sat in a chair.

The usual culprit has finished the milk.

What's that? Grace snapped.

Ann shook her head. No, she frowned. Her gaze drifted then she focused on the nurse. How did we do today?

We did our best, was the nurse's reply.

Grace Stackpole looked over her shoulder. I'm sorry, she said. What was your name again?

Ann Lord answered. It's Nora. Nora Brown. After Nurse Brown departed the room, Ann Lord said, She says she'll never leave me.

# THREE

# 8. FOG

She stood in a crowd on a mountainside in Austria. Beside her a foot taller was Ted lighting a cigarette with bare hands, his mittens on the end of his ski poles. In front of them people shuffled forward on skis a few inches at a time. A cloud blew patchily by blotting out hats and shoulders. No one spoke. Up ahead empty chairs clattered through a little shed. Now and then the machine grinded out a shriek. When a chair emerged from the shed it picked up two figures, whisking them up with a swing, then disappearing in the clouds. Ann Stackpole had on a pink parka. Why was no one talking? She looked at her husband and saw his unshaven cheek and noticed grey whiskers among the black ones, grey she'd not seen before, and suddenly had a premonition she would not see him grow old. Behind her silent figures inched forward, she inched toward the front. It was a random crowd lumped together, it didn't matter if she were with Ted or not, if she were wearing a pink parka or ermine cape or rags, if she were a woman or child or dog. It was like waiting to get into heaven.

She stood on the porch in her high heels listening to the hammering of the men building the dance floor. He came up from behind, startling her.

Don't turn around, he said.

I was just thinking about you.

You look very nice, he said. She leaned back and felt his chest against her.

She's not coming tonight, he said. The plane can't make it.

I know, she said. The fog hovered above the lawn. She felt she knew everything. Her perceptions had not changed, but they were sharper. It came from him. His chest against her shoulders. It was monumental.

*You look nice tonight they said you look beautiful I don't know what to put on* an ice-blue satin sleeveless cocktail dress a yellow coat to the knee a white shirt with the same pants *which is better the wrap or the jacket* she was walking up blue steps in a silver evening dress there was gardenia in her champagne a chiffon top gathered in the front she'd worn it in Italy but they hadn't seen it in Newport *you're all dressed up tonight* she wore pearl bracelets shoes with a squarish toe hated ruffles *should I wear it up or down I always like it up they said I like it better down* the beaded bag with beaded leaves the white linen was too summery for October *aren't you going to change* the neckline was good on her *you look beautiful they said* she could take it in at the back she didn't like it with the pockets so low it was too busy with the scarf better without the belt she should have worn the other shoes the sleeves were too tight *is that new* she changed the buttons she felt overdressed *you look perfect they said* she took off the bows the snaps went on the other side she had nothing to go with the green skirt she found the perfect grey coat couldn't bear to put the black thing on again it had had it the red dye ran in the rain her neck looked like it was bleeding they were her favorite boots they'd lasted forever the hats were just her size she bought two one black one navy had the sandals copied wrapped fur at her throat waited for them to bring the car around waited in a cloud of perfume she had only one sweater left it was a black cardigan

Ann Grant drove to the Yacht Club with Ralph Eastman. In the back sat Lizzie Tull next to Carl's friend Monty in whom she had developed a growing interest. Monty remained sphinx-like. Because they arrived on time there were no other guests save an elderly couple standing looking past each other sipping highballs. On each crowded table were the centerpieces Lila and Ann and Lizzie and Gail had gathered from the island fields—Queen Anne's lace, loosestrife, goldenrod, sweet pea, cow vetch, clover, daisies. A blue awning stretched over the deck to a white railing. Ann crossed the floor and stood looking down at the water.

A few feet out was a wall of grey fog. The water clacked under a float and rowboats which were invisible. Harris Arden, she said to herself. It was a nice name. *You look very nice.* Ann Arden. It sounded like a movie star. She knew she ought to be more distressed but nevertheless felt happy. She believed that Harris Arden's feelings for her were bigger and more important than the ones he'd had for so long with this other woman. She had nothing to support this beyond Harris Arden's sighing into her neck, she was carried by her own feeling. She'd never had such a giant emotion. It seemed a physical thing. Her instinct told her this was what one based one's life on. Lizzie Tull's laugh pierced the soft night and Ann looked back to see her eager upturned face between Ralph Eastman and Carl's friend Monty. Had any of them had such a feeling? She suspected not. Maybe one day they might. She glanced over at the man straightening bottles at the bar—she recognized him as the island electrician—and wondered if he knew the feeling. She hoped he did. And Harris? She believed he knew it now.

A wall of people dressed for evening mounted the shallow steps off the driveway, the women in belted dresses, pearl earrings and white sweaters, the men in blue blazers with brass buttons. Ann saw people she'd met over the years visiting the Wittenborns. There was Sally Thatcher whose husband had run off with a younger island girl. Seth Thatcher must have had this feeling. He and the girl were now on a boat sailing around the world. She saw the Hornblowers with their daughter Kitty in an enormous pleated dress looking more matronly than her mother. Not Kitty. The Holt brothers were shoving each other into the trophy case. She saw Ollie Granger dapper in a white dinner jacket guiding forward a small girl in a grey cocktail dress. Mrs. Wittenborn in a pale narrow sheath with jewels clustered at the neck looked the most sophisticated woman there. Her hand lingered on a man's back greeting him and Ann thought maybe Mrs. Wittenborn could be included in her group then after a moment's consideration decided it would not have been with her husband Dick. Across the room Mrs. Wittenborn caught sight of Ann, raised her glass and rolled her eyes.

The chatter increased, a few musicians in the corner started to play thumping tunes. Ann saw Lila in the teal blue dress they'd found together at Lord & Taylor with the wide straps and full skirt. Ann marveled at Lila's mixture of friendliness and reserve. How had she gotten to be so balanced? Her family teetered around her, nutty, while she had the wisdom to fall in love with the solid rock of Carl Cutler. Ann felt a surge of pride at having her as a friend. Then he was there, bigger than everyone else with eyes which saw more, wearing a not completely dark suit and white shirt and dark tie with his hair a little less sprung out than usual. Gigi Wittenborn in a daffodil yellow tea dress with fluttering sleeves and a tight low top was clinging to his arm. Had Gigi experienced the feeling? Ann shrank a little. Gigi was the feeling.

He caught Ann's eye and she saw right away the smile for her and the playful glint slightly embarrassed slightly amused having Gigi's ruffled breast pressed to his arm.

Satisfied Ann crossed the room to the bar.

I've always loved the fog, Mr. Wittenborn was saying, relieving the bartender of a brimming drink. His eyelids drooped, he wore tiny jet buttons down his shirtfront and thin needlepoint slippers on his long feet. Wonderful for the skin, he said.

Ann asked for a Dubonnet on ice and said she had a fondness for fog herself.

Mr. Wittenborn did not hear. He inhabited a solitary column unpenetrated by those around him. Through the crowd Harris Arden was making his way toward them. Ann could feel him getting nearer.

Good evening, he said first to Mr. Wittenborn, and bowed his head. Hello Ann.

Mr. Wittenborn broke out of his oblivion for one strange moment and pointed a loose finger at Harris. Why don't you marry this one? he said.

Ann looked down and blushed. The heel of her shoe wobbled and she nearly fell. Harris Arden looked at her. She sipped her drink.

Oh I'm not good enough for her, he said, holding his stare.

❊   ❊   ❊

I stopped wondering about you after a while. It took too much out of me.

If that's what you had to do, he said.

It's not what I wanted to do. The whole thing was not what I wanted.

No.

But it was the only thing. What else could I do?

Nothing. You did the best you could. We both did.

There wasn't much of a choice, she said.

We did our best.

Maybe I should have done something, she said. Maybe I could have . . .

What?

Her eyes looked this way and that. I don't know. Just not . . . I don't know. Maybe done something drastic.

Like what?

I don't know. But something. Just not let it happen the way it did.

Some things you can't help.

Think of how different it would have been, she said.

You think so?

Of course. I mean . . . She thought for a moment. I mean . . .

What?

You're right, she said. It couldn't have been different.

✿　✿　✿

The branches came in through the window, their leaves yellow and curling. They wound around the desk lamp and along the bookshelf and coiled around the bedposts. She looked up at the ceiling. There were leaves all over it. Leaves were crawling down her throat, goldenrod was shaking like a windstorm in the corner, purple lupin sprung up across the foot of the bed and ticked side to side like a metronome. Purple buds flew off into a purple tornado. But the bed remained steady, the bed didn't blow. Hope had changed direction, toward the past. Things shook through the night and at dawn she saw humming red-shelled bugs trembling on the branches as they gnawed through.

At the entrance each person took a small envelope with a sailboat embossed on it saying which number table he or she was at. The woman overseeing the seating was the same woman who organized the raffle benefits for the school. She also worked in the post office. The waiters and the people back in the kitchen all lived on the island year round. There was the boy who pumped the one gas pump carrying a bucket of ice, and the girl who worked behind the penny candy counter waiting with clasped hands by the swinging doors. All the guests being served were summer residents.

Ollie Granger stopped and introduced his girl. She had curly hair and a squinting smile and looked about fourteen except for her smoking a cigarette and wore, Ann noticed, a nice pin in the shape of a chrysanthemum.

Lily, he said, this is Ann. She's the woman I would have married if she hadn't turned me down.

Ann Grant used to see Oliver Granger at dances in Cambridge. She vaguely remembered canceling a dinner date, she'd been seeing Vernon then. Or was it Malcolm? She couldn't remember, but it was hardly a romance. But Ollie Granger was always a flirt. He was handsome in a bulldog sort of way and always flattering. At any rate Lily didn't seem in the least distressed by his comments and continued to smile at Ann.

She said hello to the Finches, an older couple she'd seen at the sailing teas. Mrs. Finch in a lavender dress leaned toward Ann and said wasn't it smart of Lila to have the dinner in this fog so not everyone could come. Mr. Finch stood by silently. She looks like a garden party, said Mrs. Finch as Gigi came toward them.

We're supposed to sit down, Gigi said, looking over their heads, searching for something.

Of course we are, said Mrs. Finch. Gilbert, do you think we'll ever find our table?

Mr. Finch scratched at his small envelope. With great application, he said, and they walked off together.

Gigi twisted around like a horse pulling at a tight bit, scanning the room, and Ann saw her eyes fire up a little when her gaze landed on Harris Arden.

Well it is her big thing, her stuff, Constance said. That's what she cared about, her house and her pictures and all her things.

I wish you would stop talking about her in the past tense, Teddy said.

She liked gardens, Margie said. Margie was now doing land-scaping work. This, after classes in anthropology, cooking school and studying sculpture.

Let's face it, she was a material person, Constance said.

Is, Teddy said.

She told me once she wanted to be a nun, Nina said. She was on the floor in black shorts and an unraveling tank top pressing her forehead to one knee then the other. The living room doors were open to the garden. Their mother had put in a fountain at the far end of the lawn which made a soothing gurgling sound when it was on, but no one had thought to turn the water on.

Give me a break, Constance said.

I'm telling you, Nina said. She said so when I was doing *Agnes of God.*

It's a knee-jerk Catholic thing, Margie said. All Catholic girls think it at some point.

I never did, Nina said, rotating her torso end extending her arms.

Do you think we should get a priest? I mean, does she want to see one? Margie said.

No one voiced an opinion.

Finally Constance said, Wouldn't she ask?

There was silence in the living room. Nina puffed in measured breaths. Then she stood up, put earphones on her ears and jogged out the door.

I think I'll call Paris, Constance said, getting up. Teddy hit a chair back and followed. Margie stood up quickly. In seconds they had evacuated the room.


Ann had Buddy on one side and Ralph Eastman on the other. Two small blue presents tied with white ribbon sat on her plate. She opened the larger, a burlap pillow with a stencil of a pinecone, hard and new. Out of Lila's hearing Gail Slater said she had three already. Lizzie Tull wanted to compare the little silver perfume flasks to make sure they were identical. Lila's initials were on one side, her bridesmaids' on the other. Harris was seated between Gigi and Gail. The wineglasses trembled in the candlelight. Buddy got up and came back, each time returning with a fresh gin and tonic.

Can I get you anything? said Ralph. He unfolded his napkin and lay it on his lap.

I'm very happy thank you, Ann said.

Yes, Ralph said. You look it.

She had known Ralph Eastman longer than she'd known the Wittenborns and it occurred to her how some people continued through no design of one's own to be in one's life while others might initially enter in a sort of blaze and seem to change everything but then might not stay around. She had never sought Ralph Eastman out, reliable Ralph with his pressed shirts and shined shoes, always on time. She did not know then what she knew now lying on her bed that she and Ralph would continue to cross paths and would know each other all their lives and his presence would turn out to be one of the more consistent threads in her life. Ralph was at two of her three weddings—no guests were at the first—he was often in Europe when she was there. He would have been at the funerals, too, though her memory of the funerals was blurred, but she could be sure of that, of Ralph Eastman's being there. In fact he and his wife Kit had been at her bedside that very morning.

The waiter put a smaller plate on top of the one there. Clams casino. Ann knew the menu.

Across the table Gigi was whispering into Harris Arden's ear. He stayed still, watching her hands move in little waves above the table, then glancing at her low neckline and cleavage. A prickly uncomfortable feeling came over Ann.

A wet washcloth scooped under her armpits. She was propped up with her head dropped forward. Her back was being rubbed.

Ted was rubbing her back, they were in a brass tub facing the same way with Ted's legs around her hips, outside was Wyoming and a ranch he was rubbing her back with soap he reached around with the soap and washed her in front he pulled her back washing slowly got under her pulled her up outside was the night deep brown and somewhere the horses they'd ridden that day and the bleached green sage and pointed peaks against the clouds the dim light sconces threw unfamiliar shadows she was splayed out new rooms inspired Ted he spread her knees her feet were balanced on the thin rim he was rubbing the bar of soap murmuring in her ear telling her what he was going to do in Ted's arms it was like being on a trip to a place she never would have gone on her own he was fierce sometimes he made low guttural sounds and afterward sitting across from him as he cut his steak it was hard to see the same man she'd seen in bed or the same power then even that changed became blunted the more he drank the more his embraces became abrupt his feeling dulled he began to panic and the more fierce he became lunging without feeling desperate to be close coming at her without warning but it wasn't working he wasn't getting through to himself he'd been padded he could not feel the softness of skin or smell her hair soon drinking was the only thing gave him a feeling and one he could count on and the lashing out came with the frustration till finally only violence provided him with genuine feeling and afterward feelings of remorse and shame and self-loathing were the only real feelings he was left with and he had not the least idea why

One night they gave a dinner and the guests took their drinks outside in the mild air and sat facing the water halfway down the long lawn. Ann Stackpole went to get more tonic and through the lit window of the kitchen saw her husband and Collie Shepley. Collie Shepley was wearing a pink sweater and Ted had his hands on her breasts. Once playing a parlor game Collie Shepley had screamed at Lizzie Brocaw for embracing Dan when they won a point. Don't you ever put your hands on my husband again! Ann walked up the steps slowly, knocking the railing, giving them time to separate and at that moment snapped off the final thread of Ted in her mind.

Though she lived on with him for a year after, imagining how it would be with him gone, not having to hear his unsteady footsteps on the stairs in the middle of the night after a visit to the liquor cabinet. So after when he was gone she thought about him little.

Smooth stones hung in the air and one by one dropped down. She'd not known how much the sound of stones clicking together meant to her till she heard them now.

Rain fell quietly outside. *Just try to eat a little.* She traveled to the other side of the bed and looked down at men working in a web of ropes and ladders with shirts off covered with sweat and mud caked at their ankles and a clanging machine at the bottom of the pit. Dishes were being stacked in the kitchen and high heels banged on a wooden porch and the *tock tock* tock of hammering went on through the night. She tried to make the pain small to keep it from invading every part *it's coming in from the south* it blew by white and all was obscured again.

She liked watching him across the table, she liked looking at the wide line of his shoulders in the dark jacket. His chair scraped back when Lila got up and scraped again when she returned. He held his fork still, listening to Buddy tell of the first time Lila brought Carl home and how they never stopped holding hands. Gigi's food lay untouched on her plate, tomato aspic, lamb chops, Dauphine potatoes. The rolls were round and hollow. The dessert plates came, whipped cream hiding the cobbler, and Ralph Eastman stood. *Tap tap tap,* silver on glass. The chatter in the room dwindled. Ralph Eastman looked down at a piece of paper.

What Ralph said was forgotten.

Mr. Wittenborn swiveled stiffly and spoke of how much it meant to be a father, never once looking in the direction of the bride. Lizzie Tull, clutching her throat and giggling, listed the names of Lila's old beaux and why each didn't deserve her. Carl's friend Monty stood up at the same time as Oliver Granger and Ollie being less gracious won out. His toast left everyone perplexed, something about Carl fixing a motorboat and not being a sailor.

Then Monty stood up and in a honeyed Southern accent said simply he wished he were marrying Lila himself.

One of the Holt boys made everyone laugh and Carl's mother spoke so softly at the far end of the room no one could hear. Gail read a rhyming poem in a shaky voice about growing up with Lila. Carl's nine-year-old nephew stood up on a chair and recited "When You Are Old" making everyone tear up. Buddy spoke robustly and thanked Carl for loving his sister and making her happy.

While Mr. Cutler rambled on Ann slipped to the corner shadows and after the raised glasses and *here heres* the musical combo started and as she had promised Lila she would Ann sang. A waiter shut off the wall lights and the candles turned the flowers into black shadows. The fog against the windows was as dense as quartz and Ann Grant sang "Our Love Is Here to Stay" in a low unhurried voice. The tables were dark islands with glowing centers and shadowy figures around them. She faced Lila and Carl's table and made out Harris Arden's brow darker than anything else in the room.

She finished, there was applause. The odd thing about applause was how sometimes it was hollow and at other times seemed to overflow. This was not hollow. Ann Grant came back to the table keeping her mouth pressed together and Lila squeezed her hand and the band launched into a lively beat. The summer residents of Three O'Clock Island were not quick to dance, they preferred to drink. A couple from Carl's side of the family not knowing any better moved into the small area cleared in front of the hopeful band and hitched their feet together in little shuffling motions. Ann thought it looked like fun but group habits are not fickle and no one joined the dancers.

He sat with her in the early evening while the nurses were changing shifts and conferring in the next room. He sat with his book shut on his knee and looked at her sleeping. Her face was altogether changed from even a few months before and he stared at it.

He had never looked for such a long time at her face and probably hadn't seen her sleeping since he was a boy standing uncertain by her bed not daring to wake her. He wondered if this would be the image which would stay with him of her mouth stretched over her teeth slightly parted and her skin smooth as china. The bones were prominent in her cheeks and the skeleton apparent beneath had the mute wisdom of a mountain range. The face had taken on something beyond the personality of his mother and the new face beneath seemed to say, This is what it comes to in the end, this is what we all are, this will come even to you.

He was not what she thought after all. Turned out Harris Arden was a superficial person who only appeared substantial. He had hardly spoken to her all night. Only when it was time to leave did he come up to her and ask her if she wanted to walk back with him. So he would see her only if they were alone? Well. O.K. she'd walk back with him, but the scales had been lifted from her eyes. He had talked with nearly everyone but her. Now what was he doing? He took the presents and tissue paper out of her hand and put them in his pocket.

In the fog the streetlights were fuzzed. The air was padded and as they walked their voices sounded strange and clear and isolated. Ann Grant walked a few feet from him with her arms folded across her chest.

That was beautiful when you sang, he said. You really should keep singing.

I would if I were good enough. I'm not.

I think you are.

You're being nice.

No I'm not. I really think so.

You're nice, she said stiffly. You're always nice.

Not always, he said. She could tell he was not thinking of her. They walked in silence.

Is something the matter? he said.

Not at all.

You seem angry about something.

She shrugged. A foghorn blew.

Then she told him in a tone which showed she didn't particularly care that she did think he'd not been very friendly tonight. When she turned to see how he'd take this he was smiling. He reached for her hand.

I was worried about seeming too friendly, he said.

Her hand remained limp.

Ann? His voice caught deep like a hook. She's coming tomorrow. I don't want it to be too awkward.

His hand was warm but she didn't hold it back.

I want her to know as soon as possible. But not here.

His warm hand was lovely.

It would be too hard. I have to wait till we get back to Chicago.

She took small steps in her heels and walked nearer to him. He was right, but she didn't have to like it. He lifted her hand to his chest. They were on a strip of road with no houses.

Ann.

I'm always in the dark with you, she said.

Will you come see me in Chicago?

I don't know.

You won't?

I don't know.

The road turned and up ahead were blurred lights with spaces between them. It was like walking on air.

You must.

She stopped and looked at him. I don't know, she said in a different way, and leaned against him. He lifted her face and turned it toward the fuzzy light coming off a porch.

God, he said looking.

He kissed her and she kissed him back.

How did this happen? he said and they kissed again.

They walked slowly and he kept his arm tight around her. They crossed the bridge at Bishops Harbor and her footsteps in heels

made the hollow sound of crossing an empty stage. She felt as if
they were made out of fog.

Come here, he said suddenly. I want to show you something. He
took her arm and led her off the road onto the gravel edge then
over the wet grass. She hoped he wouldn't let go his grip. He
brought her under a tree where the fog had not gotten to and the
night was darker and stood her against the bark. Here, he said and
pressed against her. I want to crush you.


She was pulling a rope out of the water and knew it was coming to
the end when the barnacles started to appear and they became
more thick and clustered. Then it was strangely peaceful and the
sound was turned off. She stood at the bow of a ship. If only she
could have stood this way above the water and really breathed and
let the waves go by like pages being turned and watched everything more closely and chosen things more carefully then she
might have been able to read the spirit within herself and would
not have spent her life as if she were only halfway in it.

For a moment she felt an astonishing brilliance and heat and
light and all of herself flared up and the vibration after sixty-five
years was not weakened by time but more dense then suddenly it
was as if the flame had caught the flimsiest piece of paper for it
flickered up and flew into the air then quickly sank down withered
into a thin cinder of ash which blew off, inconsequential. Her life
had not been long enough for her to know the whole of herself,
it had not been long enough or wide.


The lights were out in the big house. Everyone had gone to bed,
everyone else had disappeared. They creaked along a hall which
smelled of paint and knocked the table in the dining room jostling
the glass on the candelabra. She held his hand as he led her along,
they came out on the long porch with the black fog just past the
steps and the cushions showing striped on the chairs. He pulled

her onto a wicker couch. Come closer, he said. Come closer and he pulled her against him.

After swimming they would hang the towels over the railing here to dry. They brought out drinks and watched the sunset, they sat below the moon.

They were waiting in a transport, he told her, not sure if they'd make it out alive, they were waiting on the runway for the signal to take off. Shells exploded outside, the hull was full of wounded, packed in elbow to elbow. It was near dawn. The stretcher beside him had a man with half his face blown off so his bottom row of teeth were showing. The men were calling for their mothers, that's what they did at the end, called for their mothers. It wasn't the most danger he'd been in, but it was when he was most scared, that time. Somehow the wheels started moving and somehow they rumbled along the runway and lifted up and got out of there.

She watched the wall of fog and felt his heart against her shoulder. The fog got inside. She felt she would accomplish something in her life. She was not sure of the exact nature of what it was, but she was certain that when she came across it she would know it. There was something she was meant to do, something she was put here for. She'd not had the feeling quite like this before and having his arms around her was part of it, but not all. If she had never met him would she have felt this? She watched the curtain rise before her.


Kiss me, she said.

The man cleared his throat.

Kiss me?

Mother, it's me, it's Teddy.

Teddy, she said vaguely. Her eyes were dark buttons. Teddy. Where's Paul?

Paul's not here. It's only me.

Only you. Paul . . . She closed her eyes. If they can make it off the runway they'll bring him home in a box.

*

They lay together in the guest cottage.

How did you get to be so soft?

Is it because you're a doctor you know how to do that? she said.

It you were mine this is how I'd hold you.

That's nice.

And I wouldn't let go.

They drifted in and out of sleep.

Sometimes it's better not to do everything, he said.

It wouldn't be right I guess.

But this is, he said. This is right. You are.

She dozed on his shoulder.

How will it be when we see each other? he murmured.

Tomorrow? It will be fine.

Will it? His face was terrible.

Harris, she said. Nothing could go too wrong, nothing could ever be too bad now that she knew him. She was sure of that. That was one true thing.

After a while she said, They're flying in this morning?

He frowned in the blue light. I better be going, he said, and fell back asleep.

She saw him to the door with her nightgown wrapped around her like a sari.

It will be O.K., she said. It was the last time she felt it so absolutely, she'd yet to meet the other woman.

After he had gone she went back to bed where he'd been beside her and the place was now changed without him. She lay looking up.


There were changes in the arms which held her at night and in the profiles she made out in the dark beside her, there were different rooms and other beginnings in other beds and each time it happened there was something the same to be pressed against a new chest, to know the bright flash meeting up with the secret untapped person who appeared in kissing, who said come with me down this shadowy hall just you and I down this passage let me take you into this universe, just you and me, the face appearing up close surprising to be so near and giving her a jolt of animal fear, there was something dangerous in being so close something unnatural, but she would not run, soothed by the warmth of new hands and the swell of the new arm, not letting on kissing the new mouth which though it had familiar elements of other mouths was more new and different than familiar, would let herself be lulled, then would recognize in the eyes the drugged look of a man who thinks perhaps you are what he has been looking for and she'd think remember this look now because one day it will be gone never to appear again soon it will go and being stirred would be able to return the stare her body taken along her heart maybe a little behind while inside his head what were the mysterious thoughts his hand slipping under her sleeve sliding in and when he turned her it would be like being thrown onto a hill of soft sand her pulse speeding what else could she do now he pulled at her skirt he was removing her shoe saying what pretty feet she had his hands were trying to get in everywhere she was soft she was small she was lovely his hands were hard his breath quick on her neck what else could she do now that it had started his lips and his tongue wet and soft and wet inside it had started like a river and she would have to go the whole length of it now and who knew if it would be long or short or thick afterwards or how pale or how much pain would come it was a dark whirlpool pulling her along sweeping her she saw the secret in him the way he pulled her the way his mouth was impatient her hands were shaking her skin full of needles she felt his teeth the pool blurred around her it was past the time she might have stood apart and taken his measure now she would see him this way now he would be harder to make out she'd been swept to the other side where he came over her where he oh he had a way about him he did she went along she could only keep going could only hope as he hoisted her lifted her placed her there that he would not stop too soon that he would keep going that he would do this forever and never stop and when he did stop that they would have been carried far enough along with the water still coming beneath them and the water not stopping that it would not stop now that maybe this time there would be enough to keep carrying them enough to carry them along forever enough to make it last


She stood on a bluff above a cove of churning water. Grace Stackpole was beside her. You can't dive in, it's full of syringes, she said. Ann Lord looked down and saw they weren't syringes but martini glasses clinking together.

She heard the shouts of children in the next cove over. A stone skipped out over the flat surface.

The dull thud of stakes being hammered echoed in the still air.

It just hurts so much, she said, and immediately regretted it. Who had heard? Was it Grace or one of the children or Ollie in again? At the end of a warped lens she saw the face of Nora Brown and felt more understood by this figure in white than she had been by people she'd known all her life.

# 9. REPORT FROM NURSE BROWN

Her eyes stared ahead with pupils small dots from morphine. Nurse Brown set the tray quietly down without rattling and sat and waited. She spooned some rice and brought it to Ann Lord's lips. The lips parted but the mouth didn't open, the front teeth were set together in concentration. Nurse Brown did not like to give in to them when they refused to eat. She prodded with the spoon. Just a taste, she said. She took back the spoon and held it above her lap.

Hush, Ann Lord said.

Her face seemed to Nurse Brown as if a light had been thrown from beneath it and she saw in Ann Lord the young face she'd seen in some of the photographs around the house. There was one of Ann Lord as a young woman with her hair blowing and her teeth white in profile. Nurse Brown picked up the tray and left the room.

She sat next door in the room with the pilgrim wallpaper. In the corner was a small grey TV which she sometimes turned on without the sound while she did the crossword or looked through a magazine. The ceiling had waterstains, it was true of the best houses. She sat with the door ajar and listened as she'd listened in hundreds of other rooms with glasses gathered on bedside tables and boxes of plastic needles and checkerboard squares for pills and cotton balls and cards propped up, rooms of yellow stains and dressing gowns draped over chairs and piles of unread books. She knew that downstairs by the back door there were seamed vases from the florist empty with dry foam cubes and knew how the air in the room grew close from sleeping. A change of sheets swept hope through the room. She no longer needed to see the visitors, their voices were familiar. She knew the coats spotted with rain and umbrellas dripping in the hall and the presents tied with bows. There were silent visitors with furrowed brows, ones who didn't stop chattering, ones who whispered to her conspiratorially and ones who looked through her, she was just the nurse. Smiles might be expressions of fright. Some people with cheerful natures remained unintimidated by pain, other compassionate ones were undone. Restless people made short visits. One could only imagine how many were too uneasy to come at all. Some people were stunned and seemed oddly unmoved. The older ones were familiar with this business and their hands sat resigned in their laps and they spoke little. Children skipped in on the rug or burst into tears. Sometimes they were made to kiss the sick person which they did with trembling arms. And always there were the ones who flocked to sickbeds, regardless of their relation, the ones who brought casseroles and knocked on the door at the wrong time.

Nurse Brown saw her patient watch all this for the first time. The face propped against the pillows grew more still and watchful as the days went by till it stopped turning and soon only the eyes moved, going from one visitor to the next, watching with trepidation a cup approach.

And in the early hours of the morning Nurse Brown saw another face in the lamplight, the face wild with pain, pleading for this not to be true, a face incredulous and lost.

A nurse's first obligation was to bring comfort to the patient and there was no reason in this day and age for pain to be overwhelming. When consciousness was not engaged a patient was more susceptible to pain, so night was a critical time. Sometimes patients refused medication saying their minds were too confused. It wasn't usual but she'd seen it, some preferring pain to confusion.

Ann Lord reached for her hand. Make it go away, she said. Her hand was small and dry.

Nurse Brown bent down for a fresh needle.

No, Ann Lord said. It's over there. She pointed over Nurse Brown's shoulder. Tell it to go away.

Nurse Brown glanced behind her. It will go away when it's ready, she said.


She felt the thickness of the morphine surrounding her. Beneath it were thieves with knives ready to jab her if she dropped down so she lay very still trying not to fall through the hammock of mist holding her up and searched through herself to locate the point . . . the point was . . . but she'd lost the point. She was dissolving, only her heart was left. The world was vast and off people went and were engulfed in it and some came back and some never did. Thirty, forty, fifty years went by, at her age she could say that— fifty years. An old face might reappear, the eyes softer, the skin slack, but one could always see the earlier face. She thought of all the faces which never returned and the last times of seeing them, her mother's face twisted after the stroke, Kingie Montgomery still smoking with the tube in her throat. Some went quickly, her father, Ted, there one day then gone, and Paul . . . But she could not think of Paul . . .

She would have none of that clean break. She had not supposed the end would come for some time, she could have lived on another twenty-five years without it being remarkable. Twenty-five years more, as old as Nina. With Oscar gone she had thought glancingly of the end. She imagined it would be like standing on a plateau from which one looked down and reviewed the various roads one had traveled and saw the territory one had covered. But it was not like that. She lay looking up not down. And instead of long meandering roads and their destinations she saw a snowfall of images—faces she'd known and rooms she'd lived in and tables sat at and oceans swum in and clothes worn and streets turned onto and other beds she'd slept or lain awake in.

Her shoulders could just fit into the narrow opening but if she came off the ladder to crawl further into the shaftway she thought she wouldn't make it around the bend where it grew more narrow. She should try to go around the other way, but was there another way?

*Take this off.*

The music played in the afternoon, a foghorn sounded, no she was getting ahead of herself, rocks were clicking on a beach, a glass chandelier clicked in the dark, an old floor creaked. She rolled herself back so she wouldn't leave anything out. Sometimes time spread out like ink in water but it also had an order and one thing could not come without the other coming first.

*You have a visitor.*

A young woman held a yellow plant.

It's Can, said a high voice. Then in a normal voice, I don't know if she can hear me. Then the high voice: Hi Aunt Ann.

Lila?

It's Can. She whispered to the nurse. Can I take her hand?

Certainly.

It's good to see you, said the yellow flower.

Have you got Lila with you?

No, Mummy sends her love. They're still in Maine. She can't get around very well with the brace on, but she wants to come visit soon. She wanted me to give this to you.

We're all falling apart, said Ann Lord, smiling. Your mother carried white and blue flowers.

She did?

You're looking very tan like your uncle Buddy. He used to get black.

Yes Mummy said that too.

I hear you're getting divorced.

I am.

I guess it's what they do now,

I don't really have a choice, said Can Cutler. He left me.

A man doesn't want to hear a woman complain, said Ann. They do not want to hear your problems.

No, Can said.

I don't know if Margie learned that.

Seth had problems too I think.

They all have problems. But Constance, she learned to support herself. That's the important thing. That's the only way to be free.

Nurse Brown listened to the conversation with the door ajar.

Does she like Paris? Can said.

Ann Lord waved the subject away. So you brought in the summer with you.

Mummy said you liked begonias.

I like things hard to keep, said Ann Lord. I'll look after it for a while. She was beginning to fall asleep again.

I thought the yellow was nice.

Yellow is for heroics, she murmured. I'll give it to Constance, she's my hero.

Nurse Brown repeated this conversation to Mrs. Lord's daughter.

Constance looked wistful. Must be the drugs, she said softly.


Nora Brown was thirteen when her father got cancer. In the two years he battled it he never once complained and she took a lesson from him believing that complaining like criticizing put cracks in the world and there were enough cracks already without her adding to them. She'd chosen a profession which mended cracks. In her patients she always saw her father's face.

She entered into people's lives at the end and watched them change. Some grew more stiff, others broke apart, some spread like spilled syrup. Nurse Brown heard things brought up which had never been said before and saw new relations formed in the final hour and nearly always she made a few new ties herself.

She was a large woman with round shoulders and often wore a light blue sweater which flapped above her lower back. Her mouth slanted in and her features looked as if they were melting or shaped from melting wax. For each patient she kept a daily record in a blue notebook with a spiral binder, the sort one could always find at a drugstore.

7:15 am Patient alert Temp 98.6   7:30 Patient alert Bathe neck, face, back   8:05 ¼ cup apple juice   8:25 son TS in to visit   9:00 Morphine sulfate ½ cc as directed   9:35 ½ cup stewed prunes   10:00 change gown, care to skin   10:20 daughters Constance and Margaret   10:45 Voiding   11:00 Mr. Eastman in to visit   11:45 bowl chicken and rice soup   12 noon Morphine sulfate as directed   1:10 change position, comb hair Temp 99   2:00 apple juice

She watched people go. She once looked after a woman who was comatose for a week who opened her eyes and said, I'm coming Charlie, and that was it. Some said they really did hear beautiful music or angels singing or saw birds with swirling colors. Mostly they weren't awake at the last, they were unconscious. If they did speak it was confused. The faces were mostly resigned by then, not that they had much choice. A few might struggle against it but it was unusual to see a face in its final repose looking tortured. One saw a tortured look more often in life, one saw it on the faces of those left behind.

Patients came back. When she'd worked in the emergency room they'd bring patients back and it wasn't always the best thing. More times than not there was too much damage done. Patients said they came back after they heard people calling. *Don't leave me, Stew, don't leave me.* They said it had been pleasant in a sort of soft blackness and they would have been content to stay. But someone needed them. Floating up on the ceiling they saw themselves below on the bed being slapped and pounded on the chest while they felt calm and serene. Suddenly they'd be zapped back into their bodies and pain. They didn't know what had made them come back. They could hardly say. There was that person calling them, a child or a wife, and they felt a duty to return. They never said they came back because they wanted to live.

When the patients saw other deceased entering the room or sitting in chairs he or she wouldn't last for more than twenty-four hours after that.

Do you have a husband, Nora?

I've got Fred.

Fred Brown? Do you love him?

Sure, he's my husband. Maybe not like at first but I do.

I've had lots of husbands. It was different with each one.

That sounds right.

One could keep on having different love, if you had enough energy. It takes a lot of energy. A woman throws herself into it more than a man does, I think. She lets it take over. I let men take over my life many times. She laughed self-consciously. You must hear a lot of life stories.

Not so much. Usually sick people are more interested in what's coming for lunch.

I did, said Ann Lord. I let them take over.

But it's the women who move on, said Nora Brown. They have that. Much harder for a man to move on. Not easy for a man to change.

I don't know if I've seen that, Ann Lord said.

No, said Nora, not unkindly. You wouldn't have.

A wave of pain appeared on Ann Lord's face. Nurse Brown had seen many patients weep. It was a natural human response to pain and it was notable when she came across someone, man or woman, who did not weep. It gave you a different idea of them. Ann Lord was one of the ones who didn't weep.

One day after Ann Lord had not been out of bed for a few days Nurse Brown heard noises in the next room and stood up and listened. She didn't like to disturb a patient, a patient needed privacy as much as the next person and got it less. She heard footsteps moving across the room. She had seen patients who could not lift their hand off the coverlet one day the next day be able to walk downstairs. A piece of furniture scraped the floor, the footsteps creaked. She heard a drawer open then realized it was a window being lifted. She can call me if she needs me, Nurse Brown thought, and pulled her chair near the door. She heard a restrained groan and continued to listen as she sat down, and heard more sounds but none that Nurse Brown had not heard before.

# FOUR

# 10. The Venetian Chandelier

In the center of the ceiling was a roundish plaster mold with a pink and black glass chandelier Mrs. Wittenborn had brought back from her honeymoon. It was poignantly out of place in the little guest cottage with the molded bedposts and braided rugs and its transparent shadows looked glamorous on the ceiling. Ann Grant lay looking up at it and thought how sweet it had been with Harris Arden and went over again all the things he'd done and where his hands had been on her and saw his face and again heard his voice in her ear. She thought of their standing in the dew of the rock garden, and of the crumpling sound of sailbags, how he'd not let her turn around on the porch and of the bark pressing against her back in the fog. She felt again the jolt she got each time he'd made her feel a new thing. She relived it thinking, I will always have this, this will always be with me, his hand flat on my chest, no one can take it, I will never forget it. Nothing would alter its vividness, she would never lose it. As she went over each sensation her understanding grew of what life was for. It was for this.

She knew a change was taking place in her, she felt linked to the world. The change took place inside and no one saw it and that it happened only she knew.

Something cracked across the ceiling.

The certainty she'd felt that night remained intact. A shell had formed around it and now was cracking open. It had disappeared and yet had never gone. Was that proof of its importance or simply its lack of resolution? And what was she to do with it now after forty years? She didn't know where it came from so how could she put it back?

The house was streaming with people carrying boxes and paper bags and coffee machines into the pantry. Ann saw Mrs. Wittenborn's blue kimono flapping up the stairs. In the dining room was Buddy wearing sunglasses offering her his muffin with a bite taken out. Upstairs oblivious of the activity was Lila, the eye of the storm. Ann found her standing very still in the center of the room with her pensive expression, bottom lip cupping her top lip. The twin beds were strewn with clothes and clothes tags and tissue paper and skirts laid out. Ann pushed aside an alligator bag from a crowded armchair.

Mummy's driving me out of my mind, Lila said in a calm quiet voice.

In the next room her dress was draped like a sea monster over a chaise and hat stand and lamp.

Did you sleep at all?

I did, but I was wide awake at five. She looked into the next room. I can't wear that veil.

About when I went to sleep, Ann said.

Are you aware you have an idiotic smile plastered across your face? Lila said, relieved to change the subject.

Ann nodded.

But isn't he . . . ? Lila started shifting piles of lingerie, satin things her bridesmaids had given her which she'd probably never wear.

What?

Engaged?

Yes, but it's O.K.

Is it? Lila looked straight at Ann and for the first time Ann found Lila Wittenborn's level-headedness irritating.

Yes, it is. Insistence always had a hollow ring. I mean, it may not look that way but it's going to be fine.

There must be a better way to put it, Ann thought, she just wasn't putting it the right way.

I sort of thought he was flirting with Gigi, Lila said, picking up a peach bedjacket.

More like Gigi flirting with him.

Oh, Lila said.

Li, said Ann.

Then that's good. Lila inspected the quilting on the sleeves.

This is big, Ann said.

Lila put down the jacket and sat on the bed. I like Harris. I think he's great. She took a deep breath. But I also think that—

Lila! Her mother called from the hall.

What?

Mr. Conti's here!

Lila looked at Ann. The hairdresser, she said.

Ann didn't stand up right away, suddenly feeling her lack of sleep.

❀   ❀   ❀

Could she sing?

A little.

She could? She could sing?

Not like you.

She was pretty though, and had style. I could see how you'd fall in love with her on a tramcar. I wonder if you would have fallen in love with me on a tramcar. I doubt it.

I don't.

I wouldn't say I was at my best on a tram.

I would have fallen in love with you anywhere.

I was hoping she wouldn't be pretty and then she arrived looking so stylish. I mean, not too chic but with a style. She had good taste, didn't she.

So do you.

Hers was classic.

It was different.

Well, it was her job after all, she said. Fashion.

She was good at her job, he said.

Right away I could see why you liked her. I don't know if that made it better or worse.

I hope it made it easier, he said.

Darling nothing made it easier.

❁   ❁   ❁

They were on the driveway unloading the car. Through the wavy glass of the hall windows one could see the blue bay. Ann came up slowly from the cottage and saw a woman with short dark hair leaning on a railing with a sweater thrown over her shoulders. She was looking up at Harris and smiling.

She said hello to the Tobins first. At another time they would have kissed Ann hello, now they merely shook her hand. Mr. Tobin didn't seem to remember who she was, but Mrs. Tobin did. Ann was the one who'd thrown her son over. Spring Tobin, Vernon's little sister, gave Ann a tight hug, holding no grudge.

Ann stepped up on the porch.

Maria, this is Ann, Harris said. He had his hand on Maria's shoulder. The woman leaned forward smiling with a dark red painted mouth and shook hands and leaned back closer to Harris.

You finally made it, Ann said not looking at Harris.

It took us a while. Her eyebrows went up. She had a high voice. Her posture was good, like a dancer's. Things always go wrong when I travel, she said smiling at Harris. Ann looked for something wrong in her. Wasn't her head a little big? Her eyes a little close together?

Aren't you going to say hello?

Ann turned around to the abrupt face of Vernon Tobin. Vernon was her same height so she always felt as if she was looking down at him.

Vernon, how are you? She kissed him on the cheek and started to introduce him to Harris and Maria but of course they all knew each other. Vernon stared at her.

How are you? he said in dull tones.

Very well.

You look well. And New York, how is it?

Good. It's New York.

Not a place I could live, Vernon said.

I know. Vernon had been clear about his opinion of New York.

So, he reported, we stayed last night at the Blue Hill Motel. Spring and I shared a room, and Maria was sick all night.

Oh no. Ann looked at Maria who was still smiling.

I feel better now, she said.

Vernon went on. We think it was the clams. None of us got sick, but Maria must have gotten a bad clam. He continued to stare at Ann.

The last time she'd seen Vernon Tobin had been the winter night at the Ritz when they'd met for a drink. She'd broken off with him a few months before and they'd exchanged a few stilted letters and when he heard she was up seeing Lila he wanted to see her, there was something he needed to clear up. They met in the upstairs lounge. Vernon talked about common friends and about a trial filling the newspapers and while he was telling her about changing offices at the bank he slipped something out of his pocket and put it down on the low table in front of them next to the silver bowl of nuts. It was a square velvet box. Her heart began pounding in a sort of sickened way. He continued talking about a new person they'd hired whom he'd known at prep school. He did not mention the box.

Vernon, she said finally. What's that?

Look and see.

She picked up the box and opened it. Vernon, she said not happily.

It's a ring.

Yes I see.

It's for you.

Vernon—

Do you like it?

It's very pretty, but Vernon—

It's an emerald.

I know. Ann did not touch it. On either side of the emerald were diamonds. It was tilted into the little ring slot. It was a very nice ring. She was surprised Vernon had come up with such a good ring.

I'm glad you like it. His shoulders were hunched, braced for a blow and he was rubbing one hand with the other. He didn't look at Ann. Try it on, he said.

Vernon, I can't take this.

I want you to marry me, he said. He spoke so softly she could hardly make out the words, but she knew what they were.

We haven't been seeing each other. I thought you understood that I—

I take it that's a no? He still didn't face her.

I'm sorry. She closed the box and held it out to him. It's beautiful though.

He looked at the box. I don't want it.

Vernon.

You keep it. I don't want it. What do I want with an emerald ring? Nothing believe me.

Return it, she said. Or give it to . . . another girl.

He looked at her now. I got it for you.

Yes but it's an engagement ring. I can't keep it if we're not engaged.

Then don't think of it as an engagement ring. If that's what's stopping you.

She put the box down on the table.

Vernon looked impatiently for the waiter and quickly paid the bill. They took their coats from the backs of the armchairs and stood up. Ann started to walk away.

Are you going to leave your ring there? he said.

She turned around, buttoning her coat. Vernon.

What.

I can't take the ring.

His mouth was pinched. Then I guess no one will, he said and swept past her. She hurried after him and caught up with him on the white curved staircase.

It's still there, Vernon.

He didn't stop. She followed him down through the lobby and out the revolving doors to the sidewalk where it was cold and dark blue, and dirty snow was heaped on the curb.

Vernon, I'm sorry. She reached for his shoulder.

He turned around. There were wet streaks on his face. He wiped them with a flat palm, and his gaze shot upward to the windows of the lounge where they had sat, considering something— how things might have gone otherwise—thinking what he left behind.

A freckled woman came out on the porch, smoking.

*This* is Kingie, Vernon said as if the subject had already come up.

Hi. The woman said, frowning and tilting her mouth. She sucked on her cigarette and glanced critically around. So this is Maine, she said.

Kingie's from Memphis.

Nice to meet you, Ann said.

Kingie nodded. She'd think about that later.

I might go lie down before lunch, Maria said, and Ann saw her gaze at Harris.

They walked together down the lawn. Harris carried Maria's bag.

Harris! Gigi burst from a screen door. Aren't you playing tennis with us?

Not wanting to shout Harris turned and walked back to Gigi and Ann saw that he was a man women sought out. *How will it be when we see each other . . .* She'd not met his eye all morning.

After conferring with Gigi Harris returned to Maria who slid her arm around his. They went past the red barn over the black shadows on the grass toward the children's house. Maria's navy blue sweater slipped and he caught it, and Ann found herself watching the man she loved adjust the sweater on the shoulder of his fiancée and seeing her slender ankles at the end of her slim pants as they passed by the red barn and over the green grass. Why was it this man? It could have been anyone. Two days ago she didn't even know him. Why wasn't he someone else. Like so many things in life there was no explaining it.


*I love you. Very much.*

Wait. Which one was that. It was snowing in the canals, it was Venice. Was it Oscar or Phil? Not Ted. It was January and snowing and snowflakes drifted down and disappeared in the green water. Warm me up, she said. There was a long warm body and fresh cotton cold at first and the bed made tight and a tray of coffee. *Warm me up* It was Phil who liked the neatness of hotel rooms and grew irritated as the packages collected and the maps were spread out on the bed. He was proud of bringing her to Venice first and watched her face. *Phil Phil warm me up* She wished she could have loved him better, her heart when she met him was shut like a safe, and having the girls didn't help, she stayed home and he went to his clubs, so when he turned to other arms she could not blame him. Summer heat blew up from the lapping alley below and it was Venice with Oscar standing again at a latched window, he said you need to get away, but she should not have left the children so soon, she should not have left Teddy, she should not have been without the girls. There had even been a Venice with Ted who was impatient in the dark churches, preferring Harry's Bar morning noon and night.

They all took her to Venice. It was full of water, each time full of a grieving water, increasing, the quiet clopping of the streets at night. And Phil came back to her watching her face when the window swung open with the snowflakes when he saw that she did not need him the way he hoped she would, that she was sealed off from him and he could not warm her. She should not have gone back, it belonged to a place where she should never have gone. Venice, so beautiful everyone said, ah my favorite city. Venice was children left behind, children gone, it was love not found, it was love missing. She was stupefied in Venice, breathing loss. Venice. Everyone talked about it and everyone adored it. She wished she'd never seen the place.

Constance Katz gave the short version of her romantic crisis. She'd kicked out Luc who said his affair with his photography assistant was a passing thing and she should just be patient.

If you want him, her mother said, you can get him back.

It's not that simple.

I'm afraid it is.

Mother, you don't know.

I know more than you think, Constance.

It was not easy to argue with a woman lying motionless under the covers. You don't know Luc, Constance said.

They're all little boys, said Ann Lord. If you really want him back, treat him badly.

Great, Mother.

Treat him badly and he'll come back. I promise.

Is that how you got Papa back? Constance said, folding her arms.

Sweetheart, you know I didn't want him back.

She dreamed every ring she'd ever worn had left its imprint on her fingers and she could see the traces of all of them, the oval ring with the seal, her mother's sapphire, the jeweled guard rings, the square diamond from Oscar, the three opals in a row, the enamel dome, the Plexiglas cube, the gold wedding bands. Each time a ring was put on her finger she'd had the illusion of safety. If you believed in safety you were more likely to find happiness. In the dream it was the impression the rings had left, not the rings, which remained. They left their imprint the way kisses did not. They left an imprint while the impression left by a man's arms worn around one's body night after night for years was not left.

She woke and thought of what was left. She had always believed in the accepted wisdom that what was important would endure and in the end survive and what mattered would last and be recognized and saved. But she saw now that was not true.


Ann Lord's children sat in the kitchen drinking tea.

I think she's gotten sweeter, Margie said.

I wouldn't go that far, Constance said, turning the pages of a newspaper and not reading. It's just the drugs.

Lauren thinks she's gotten nicer, Teddy said.

Constance became interested in an article and folded her arms on her lap and lowered her profile nearly touching her chin to the table.

Is Lauren coming over? Margie said.

She's bringing the girls.

Is that a good idea, do you think?

They don't have to go up, Teddy said.

I didn't mean that. I just meant Mother might not be up for it.

Then they don't have to go up. Lauren doesn't think it's probably very good for them anyway.

Kids can handle more than you think, Constance said.

She's just being protective, Teddy said.

Constance looked up. All these things that Lauren thinks, she must be a lot more talkative than when she's around us.

She is. Teddy poured his tea down the sink. His footsteps were firm going down the hall.

Lauren's pretty talkative around me, Margie said. She's not that quiet.

Whatever. Constance closed the paper. She's not being particularly more sweet to me, though. Mother.

What? She said you were heroic, Margie said.

I think the nurse got it wrong, Constance said.


They were drinking coffee on the porch and Ann took the baby out of Oscar's arms to find a place for her to nap. The Montgomerys' house was full of house guests and she walked past the tall pillars with the French doors open to the rows of rooms. She took the steps at the end and carried the baby through the shade of the hanging moss to the old slave quarters which Kingie had converted into guest cottages. Ann walked to the last one which she'd been told was empty and when she stepped into the small kitchen was seized with a tightening in her chest at the smell of the pipes and rust and remembered before she knew what it was some powerful thing and going into the bedroom was further struck when she looked up and saw a black and pink Venetian chandelier hanging over the bureau. It was the Wittenborns' wedding present to Kingie and Monty. She put the baby down and stood transfixed looking at the glass drops only dimly remembering where they were from feeling she was seeing something of herself which she had lost long ago.


Then came a mercifully peaceful day with nothing stirring. Her body felt lighter, there was less of her. It was very still, the water was still as glass. Almost too quiet. She used to have days when she'd go into town, she used to meet women for lunch on fogged winter days, she gave birth, she gave birth again, she kept the children from—no she could not keep them. No. There was a call from Virginia. No one would have ever dared make that call. They came and found them on the boat, it was full of wind but the sound stopped, the wind was wild, everything was flapping. The Coast Guard came and at first everyone on board joked about being arrested for dropping over the empty vodka bottles but it turned out they were looking for someone, they were looking for the Lords. Oscar turned and watched her, she was coming up from below, and after that nothing more could happen in her life. She could not look at anyone, she could not believe it. She could not look at Teddy after that, Teddy with the same face only not as thin. Nothing happened after you lost your son then before she knew it she was pregnant again at her age which could not happen either and Nina came . . . oh who? Who was that? *I can't stay long* It was Ralph Eastman in a dark suit.

He had stopped by after business in New York and was off to West Africa again before returning to London. He had married Fiona Speed's sister Kit who sent her love and he made Ann Lord laugh describing Fiona's weekend parties. Then his voice changed.

I have to go.

Yes. She smiled.

Off on this tour.

Great smile on her tight-skinned face.

I'll be thinking of you, he said.

And I'll think of you.

On my travels. He gazed at her, his old friend.

On your travels. She held her smile.

Being led around . . .

Yes.

By my nose.

By who knows.

Yes, by who knows.

Her jaw once round was now sharp like a shovel.

Well then, he said and kissed both her cheeks.

She still smiled. I don't know what to say, she smiled.

Nothing you need to say.

She held that smile. Ralph Eastman was not smiling.

Good-bye Ann.

Good-bye Ralph.

He stood and picked up his folding bag which for some reason he had carried all the way up the stairs with him to her room. His briefcase he'd left downstairs in the hall.

What are the paper plates for? she said.

What's that?

She shook her head. He slung the bag over his shoulder. Her face looked grey in the light. He would never see her again.

That's it, she said, still smiling, and there was nothing left for him to do but depart the room.

# 11. FASTENING THE SUSPENDER

A knock on the door. She was still trying to do something with her hair. Ann Grant opened the door and found Buddy Wittenborn on the step looking past her.

I can't do this, he said, and held up a white suspender with a leather buttonhole shaped in a Y. He turned around.

She found the buttons tucked in the waistband at the curve of his back. What would you do without me? she said.

His ear was tilted back to her, but he did not turn or answer. His eyes out of the side of his glasses were solemn and she never forgot the way his head was bent and how nothing was said. It was his sister's wedding day. She buttoned the button into the buttonhole and thought of how they were all there for Lila and Carl and how each of them was a part of it and they were all a part of each other.

✻

Phil Ted Oscar

They all said will you marry me it had been raining they were by the river another couple walked by a boat slid past in the dark like a jeweled cuff Phil took her by the collar I want to marry you they said they stopped dancing and stepped onto the porch by wisteria vines she was glowing she felt herself glow Ted whispered in her ear I have decided not to let you go they sat at a table in the awning shade the bell tolled the pigeons flew up Oscar poured wine into her glass and put the bottle down will you they said would you marry covering her hand with their hand by the olives on the plate and the slices of bread I do not want to live without you they said I want to live it with you their eyes were ready to jump off a cliff I always wanted I never thought I always hoped they took her in they took her by the elbow they took her in the dark she was a surprise they stood at the door when she opened it they were on the other end of the phone they mused in a half-light I never thought they said she fit herself under their arms she fit herself underneath she fit herself alongside them and did not think how she got there did not think when a new one came how the others faded she remembered the ones before but not how she had fit alongside them that was blotted out with the new face and the new form would you mind if I oh that sinking feeling oh here we go again they kissed her in a taxi they kissed her against a shadow they kissed her on the wet sidewalk against a car she was wearing her little grey coat they buried their face in her neck she could smell the wisteria with its winding trunk the music was still playing they took her hand on a narrow street pulled her near the stones under her feet were uneven they were sunk against a red chair in the study their hair was brown their hair was black in the foyer their hair was white their fingers were big can I they said can I do you know how nice that is let's not stand here is there someplace I can can I come up do you think that I that depends could you ever be do you wonder that depends I would like to spend it with you I will always I will never I know I am young and don't know I know I am not so young anymore I will always I will never tell me again of course I do by now

you should know don't you know by now of course I do I know I do
too they all said they would they all said they did they all said I do


Lila's room was crowded with her skirts, her veil, her mother and
five bridesmaids all in the same foam green dress. Perfume min-
gled with powder. On Ann the bridesmaid's dress looked handsome, on Gigi monumental. Gail Slater was a tall blade of grass in
it and Eve Wittenborn lying on the chaise with her feet up was
curvy like an inchworm. Lizzie Tull's dress was loose in the straps
and snug in the torso cutting into her skin. She was placing the veil
combs in different positions on Lila's head. Mrs. Wittenborn
leaned on a windowsill, cigarette near her mouth, studying her
daughter. Gigi was at the window looking down at the driveway.
There go the boys, she whispered.

The veil sprouted up from Lila's head. It looks so pretty, said
Mrs. Wittenborn.

The bridesmaids were silent. Lila's hair had been done by Mrs.
Wittenborn's hairdresser from Boston in a sort of puff, a way she
never would have worn it before and would never wear it after.

At the last minute Lila asserted herself and refused the veil.

They arrived at the church in the buggy and the horse got
spooked and nearly knocked the carriage over. Lila was unfolded
from the cab and her skirts fluffed out. Mr. Wittenborn stood by in
a cutaway with vest and top hat. Lila stepped into position inside
the door, assuming her role with an ease which surprised Ann
Grant. Her face had not the least trace of self-consciousness. Gigi,
a foot taller in her green high heels, gravitated to the ushers and
was examining the lily of the valley in Harris Arden's lapel.

The church was full. An organ played mournfully.

A car pulled up and spilled out a couple with a baby pulling off
caps and removing sweaters. Ralph Eastman led them to a bench
in the rear.

Who was that?

Carl's cousin Esther, said Lila staring ahead.

Ann recognized the couple who'd danced the night before at the Yacht Club. The woman gazed about cheerfully then stood up and made her husband follow in mortification carrying blankets and bottles and stuffed animals as she scurried to a better position in the front and settled down. The organ paused and the wedding march began.

At the altar the ushers stood in a line, Ralph Eastman, Harris Arden, Carl's brother Pip, Carl's friend Monty, and Buddy as best man beside Carl who stood with hands folded in front of him and watched as the bridesmaids came one by one down the aisle carrying trembling bouquets. Then came the flowergirl Spring Tobin wearing a lopsided wreath of roses clutching a basket of ivy. The bridesmaids lined up opposite the ushers and Ann saw Carl's face change when he caught sight of Lila. He watched her float toward him on her father's arm as if this were a private moment between them with none of the surprise or fear or self-satisfaction one saw in many less happy couples. Ann had seen many brides white as ghosts but Lila's color was high. She met Carl's eye not smiling then when she reached him smiled and he smiled back.

Who gives this woman to be wed?

Mr. Wittenborn staring into the mid-distance unwrapped Lila's arm. I do, he said. He bowed forward, then stepped back handing her over to the care of another man.

The priest cleared his throat. Ann Grant looked at Harris Arden opposite. He winked.

Later Lila would say she didn't remember one moment of the ceremony.

As Ann walked down the aisle hooked to Ralph Eastman's arm she looked around for Maria di Corcia and saw her beneath a large navy blue hat with pearls around her neck. She looked very pale and Ann had to admit glamorous.

They stepped outside into the bright dappled shadows. Harris Arden stood there a head above her as people streamed by and car doors slammed. He looked down. Which car are you in? he said, but the way he stared at her seemed to mean something else. He was looking into her face and past it and beyond into something way back in her. Herself.

In the closet down the hall and back deep in the closet off her bedroom were the dresses she'd worn to all the weddings. The navy suit with the white trim to Constance's at City Hall and for Margie's in the field on Three O'Clock Island the dark flowered one with elastic sleeves. For Teddy's in the little town in North Carolina where Lauren was from the purple silk with the straw hat. At her own she'd always worn white. Phil had the little white suit and Ted the long one with the train and for Oscar the lace one he picked out with the scooped neck. She liked putting on a dress with a man in mind. She'd given the flowered one to Margie who'd cut the skirt and let the hem unravel.

❖    ❖    ❖

Were you thinking of me then?
    Of course I was.
    In the church.
    It was hard not to think of you.
    But you had someone else to think of too, didn't you?
    I did.
    She was there first.
    She was.
    Is getting there first so important?
    It can be, he said.
    Is it really the important thing? People give it a lot of importance. They give a lot of importance to time, don't they? As if time added up to something.
    Doesn't it?
    She shook her head.

❖    ❖    ❖

Rounded cars parked in the lumpy field, the music of the band came over the grass and further back was a field where it was quiet behind the trees. Ann Lord had not thought of that field then, of the quiet field where no one walked, but she thought of it now.

Haze was glowing like a white ball at the horizon. A line snaked up to the couple, to Mrs. Wittenborn in pale yellow, to Mr. Wittenborn turning back to his drink on a table within arm's reach. Carl's parents stood beside, smaller and softer and wider, shaking with both hands. Buddy crossed the dry field swinging a bottle of champagne and Eve Wittenborn was applying lipstick in a sideview mirror. Above the tent on the rise stood Ralph Eastman, Pip Cutler and Carl's friend Monty each holding a drink, talking as men do, not looking at each other, surveying the scene before them. Ann saw Vernon Tobin's hand on Kingie's back trying to steer her in one direction while she veered vaguely off in another and there was Ollie Granger's fiancée Lily comparing engagement rings with Charlie Elisofen's fiancée. She saw—

Mrs. Lord. I'm sorry. Mrs. Lord.

The sun went behind a cloud and the field went dark in a vast bruise. The trees stood straight and dark at the edge and a shadow leapt out across the bed and monkeys started swinging on a sagging rope above her. Then there wasn't a rope and the monkeys were still swinging and she didn't know why they didn't fall and land on her face.

I've told you to call me Ann, Nora.

We've got to change the sheet, Ann.

She rolled over.

She stood at the bottom of the field and saw them at an upper split rail fence, he was beside the girl in the blue hat. A thin scarf around her neck was lifted by the wind. She leaned forward like a seasick passenger on an ocean liner. His arm curved over her. Ann jumped when Lizzie Tull knocked her with an elbow.

He's not the man for you, Lizzie said. She shook her head matter-of-factly, and cast an indifferent look in the direction of the couple at the split rail fence. Ann continued after that to be friends with Lizzie Tull who went on to marry an irritating man named

Brocaw, but she never lost the feeling after that moment that Lizzie Tull had not the slightest idea who she was.

Gigi joined them, dripping champagne onto Ann's shoes. She looks like a mannequin in a store window, she said.

Some men like that, Ann said uncertainly.

Gigi narrowed her eyes. I'd marry him too, she said.

She still looks unwell, Ann said.

I hope so, Gigi said, and threw her champagne glass into the tall grass at the edge of the field.

Lila and Carl danced their first dance. Everyone applauded. Across the floor of the tent Ann caught Vernon Tobin regarding her with the intense one-eyed stare he got after a few drinks. She looked away. Couples stepped onto the dance floor, feeling jaunty. The setting sun came over the rim of the hill lighting up the far side of the tent a tarnished orange, picked out the dancing figures so parts of them looked dipped in copper.

❀   ❀   ❀

Hope is a terrible thing, she said.

Is it?

Yes, it keeps you living in another place, a place which doesn't exist.

For some people it's better than where they are. For many it's a relief.

From life, she said. A relief from life? Is that living?

Some people don't have a choice.

No and that's awful for them.

Hope is better than misery, he said. Or despair.

Hope belongs in the same box as despair.

Hope is not so bad, he said.

At least despair has truth to it.

You're in a dark mood today.

She tried a smile. It's all this time I spend with my eyes shut. She closed her eyes. I stopped hoping with you right away.

Did you?

I had to. Of course the shock helped.

Yes the shock.

Some of them never got over it, you know.

Forgot it, you mean?

I suppose that's what I mean, she said. Some of them never forgot it.

❊   ❊   ❊

The band took a break while everyone found the right seat for dinner. A scratchy record played some Bach chosen by Mr. Wittenborn. The bridal table was the last to be seated. Lila was in conference with her mother whose perturbed look reflected a growing awareness of her daughter's independence. Carl waited for his bride standing beside his chair and watched calmly as she wove her way through the tables and was stopped at every turn. Ralph Eastman also stood. Buddy sat back sprawled in his seat having pulled Gail Slater's chair close to his. Monty watched his sleeve which Lizzie Tull was poking with little jabs.

They'd finished the first course when Harris joined them and filled the empty place beside Ann.

I'm so sorry, he said to Lila. Maria's feeling awful. She's upset she's missing the reception.

Lila smiled broadly. That's O.K. I mean that's too bad, but it's O.K.

Did she throw up more? Lizzie shouted.

Harris glanced at her. She's lying down, he said softly.

Lucky she has a personal doctor, Gigi said.

Harris Arden's face was pinched. He looked down at his plate of food and reached for a drink. The table returned to general discussion.

Everything O.K.? Ann said.

He looked at her, the look seemed to hurt him. I'll tell you later, he whispered.

The band started up and people stood to dance between courses.

Will you dance with me? Ann said.

He stood up.

His arms went around her easily and the music was not fast or slow and she felt something languid and warm come over her and had to keep checking herself not to fall into a revery and sink against him. He had a firm hold and moved her and her feet seemed to float where he led.

Are you worried about her? Ann said into his ear.

Not now.

Was that, don't ask now or no I'm not worried now? He shifted his hand to envelop her hand in his. She felt the pressure of his other hand on her back. He turned her a little this way, a little that. He stepped her back suddenly and it seemed to flip her into another dimension. Her forehead rested on the skin above his collar.

Ann, he murmured.

Through his shirt she could feel his heart beating. Or was it hers? The song ended and immediately went into another and they danced the next song, not speaking. When the music stopped she heard clapping around her and stood in front of him limp and radiant.

I better go check on her, he said.

It was like a stab. She smiled nevertheless. He walked head bowed off the dance floor.

Night fell suddenly and the striped light of the tent became a lantern one. The cake was carried out on a table and Lila and Carl fed it to each other with their fingers. Lila's hair had come unraveled and she looked herself again.

I'm glad that's over. It was like a job, she said. Carl was behind her talking to his cousin and Ann saw how he and Lila were joined but separate and wondered if Lila had found a superior love. Ann's idea of love had to do with merging and at the moment she thought nothing could be greater than that overwhelming feeling.

He was gone a long time.

Ann danced with Buddy till he fell down, then with Ollie Granger after he cut in on her and Ralph Eastman. Ollie had flair and twirled her around, making a space in the center of the dancers. She danced with Carl who was making sure to dance with each bridesmaid, though his eye always followed Lila. Ann kept glancing out into the dark. Still he didn't come. Some older guests left. Mr. and Mrs. Wittenborn danced with each other, looking over each other's shoulders, holding on as if they were strangers. Ann danced with a blond man who asked for advice about his girl-friend and Ann found herself feeling wise and she asked the man questions about love and how he felt and answering them for her-self passed the test with Harris and felt this man, this blond man whose name she did not know, was just another element pointing her toward Harris and she felt she gave him something back too, whoever he was, and he nodded thoughtfully. She danced with Buddy again during a slow song and he leaned against her. Do you remember when we stole the plums? he said, and she looked up and was surprised by the eyes looking at her which if she had not known better would have said were full of meaning. But she did know better, Buddy had been drinking for days. She returned her cheek to his shoulder and he stopped moving and stayed still and she felt a sudden disturbance which it was hard to know if it was good or bad. I better go, he said, and left her alone on the dance floor trembling a little.

Then Harris appeared out of the darkness. Before he saw Ann he was whisked along by Gigi who ignored his worried look and pulled him by the arm over to the band where his face lit up with relief as he strapped on a saxophone handed to him by one of the band members. He stayed off to the side and Ann saw a new aspect to him as he pressed the keys and stood with his neck hung for-ward. The music came out smooth and humming and she felt the vibration in her rib cage. He straightened up then bent back and hit a high note which he held and held till someone hooted and everyone started clapping.

In no time the dance floor was swirling. Lizzie Tull pulled Monty over and Gail Slater's sharp elbows jutted upward and Buddy hopped like a pogo stick. Ann was swept in and twirled around and through the figures saw Harris clasping the saxophone concentrating and the music spread out into all of them. Buddy's shirttails were untucked and Lizzie's straps fallen. Vernon Tobin stamped his feet as if he were killing bugs and Kingie swung side to side gazing mutely upward. Ralph was not so overcome that he didn't pause to right an overturned glass on a table but his shirt was soaked through. Carl had Lila pulled close with her skirt swelled out behind and they rocked at a slower tempo. People glanced over, proprietary, and Harris kept playing.

While Ann was growing up her mother often repeated to her, Don't be absurd. Sometimes the phrase was Don't be ridiculous. Don't be absurd usually followed an expression of emotion from Ann. In order to spare herself the embarrassment of emotion Ann had learned to rein in the expression of feelings and eventually the feelings themselves, treating them as if they were unruly children who ought to be tamed instead of allowing them free expression as a sort of fuel drawing her into life. On this night in July that habit of control was challenged by the music and the dancing in the lantern light of the wedding tent. The feeling she had was too great to check and she did not check it. The music howled in the night.

You were great, she said.
  Thank you.
  You really were, great.
  Thank you really. He ran his hand through his hair. Can we talk somewhere?
  Yes.
  At the cottage?
  O.K.
  In fifteen minutes?
  She nodded.
  What is it? he said.
  Nothing.
  Ann?

I'm sorry. I just—

I know, he said. I'm the one who's sorry.

She looked away from him. I just don't like it, she said.

I know. It shows.

What?

In your mouth. It shows around your mouth. He was smiling for the first time all night.

She pressed her lips together. I'm not sure I like that.

You can't help it, he said. Then his figure was engulfed in the darkness beyond the tent and Ann stood with a heart having grown huge and wide and felt most of it go into the dark with him.

The musicians were packing up and Ann went over to the band-leader who was red-faced from his exertions.

She went over with her big heart. I wanted to thank you for the wonderful music. She put out her hand.

I don't shake hands with girls, the bandleader said, and he kissed her on the mouth.

She heard something soft on the rug in the hall. *Please don't be anyone. Don't come.* They mustn't come yet. She could not have them here with their eyes asking. She could not answer anymore. She could not answer their eyes. She could not have them pressing near. She could not even say no. She could not be where they were.

They bent down and she knew what they saw, the dent she made in the bed, the shrinking dent. She was growing smaller and smaller. She couldn't help it and she couldn't help them. She couldn't help anything anymore. She didn't want to see their worry. She wanted them to go away and yet wanted them near. She wanted his hand, she wanted someone to take her hand and take her away, but he was not there and all the someones were gone.

Small flames in paper bags flickered on the dark lawn. Above in Lila Wittenborn Cutler's room the bride was changing into her traveling suit for the drive to the inn less than a mile away. In the morning she and Carl would fly off to another island, a brighter palmier one in the Caribbean.

One after the other the bridesmaids embraced Lila. Then Lizzie Tull pushed Ann Grant and Gail Slater out of the room so Gigi could have a last moment with her sister. The three green attendants clipped their way down the back stairs of the bright empty house into the bustling kitchen where glasses were being dried and fitted into cardboard boxes and the top of the wedding cake with the spun sugar birds attached cheek to cheek was being wrapped for the freezer. A woman with a red nose scrubbed in a foamy sink and two stooped boys carried a crate. The girls swept through the pantry where a man was stacking wine bottles and a woman in an apron scraped food into a bin through to the hallway with the hooks and into the larder where a lightbulb blazed. On the shelf beside the gold-labeled marmalade and rusted tea tins and cans of potato sticks sat the boxes of rice.

Lizzie was saying, I found out that his real name is Volentine Montgomery.

No wonder he goes by Monty, said Gail.

Shadows stretched from the milling figures and threw bars of light over Lila and Carl as they ran down the slope in a hail of rice to the car. Silhouetted in the doorway behind stood Gigi with red eyes looking rapt and lost. The last thing Ann saw of Lila was her calf and the navy blue shoes they'd bought together at Bonwit's pointed into the driveway dirt before being tucked up behind the door. Buddy held onto the handle and ran alongside the car as it went faster and faster till he could hold on no more and had to let them go.

# 12. THE WEDDING NIGHT

*She was being twisted this way and that a man was twisting her there were hands and arms turning her and old stirrings and they were all echoes of the first strong one the time when all of her was there engaged and all the ones after were references to that so as she lay on this white leaf nearly transparent and felt again the dark hill where she'd lain and finding it still there thought what else had she known but his voice his shadow his skin his look at me, his hands on her waist and how quiet he was in love what else had life been but a night in the dark on the ground turning in a stranger's arms*

Is that you?

His head was a dark shape against deeper darkness and his white shirt was solid when she touched it.

There's someone in there, he said.

A flash of green went by the cottage window.

Gail, she said. He touched her arm loosely then his fingers fell. So he's come from the other one, Ann thought. She did not want to talk about that or to think about it or to know anything of it. So she said, How is she?

Sleeping.

She alright then? The words dropped dull as stones. She dropped small stones on the subject of Maria.

The screen door opened above them and Gail came out in slacks. She saw Ann and Harris in the darkness and walked by matter-of-factly saying, Now I feel normal again, and left them alone, something which made Ann always love her. But Ann didn't care so much if they were seen together. It was past that now.

Then Gigi appeared out of the dark, breathless. We're going to the Plunge, she said, pulling at Harris and her head tilted as she took in Ann's position beside Harris. In a level voice Harris said, We'll meet you there, and she sprung back as if he'd given her a shock. She ran up through the striped shadows in her bare feet and looked back once as if to remember something then turned forward, hair streaming behind. Buddy standing with the others near the truck called down, Forget you two! He made the motion of throwing a ball. Ann remembered that. *Forget you two.*


This was the last story she'd ever tell.


He took her hand and they started across the field then turned down the dirt drive with the grass in a darker strip sprouting up the middle.

I have something to tell you.

He was solemn. But if it came from him, she thought, it could only be good, and she didn't worry. His hand was in hers and as long as his hand was in hers she could hear anything. She was thoroughly strong with his hand. She waited.

O.K., she said, and still he did not speak.

They walked through a dark patch of trees and suddenly a branch creaked and something whooshed over their heads. It swooped near flapping silently into the dark. Ann knew: it was the owl, she told him an owl lived there. She stayed near to Harris, touching him. He said he'd never seen an owl before and stopped walking and stared into the black place where the branch had sprung. Not that I even saw that one, he said. His voice was worn out.

She walked beside him feeling the pebbles through the soft soles of her shoes and her heel grinding the dirt. Light from the tent lit up the field to their right like theatre lights reflected from a stage cutting the trees around the edge in half with shadow and still he didn't say anything. He was troubled. Whatever it was, she thought, I won't think it so bad. It wasn't always obvious what other people cared about or wanted or how other people would react to the same thing or what would make people happy or what they wouldn't like. Often something mattered a lot to another person which was hardly anything to you, often you were surprised.

She said his name to herself and felt it inside her as something full. Harris.

Can we get to the water from here? he said.

Yes, there was the Lorings' dock and she led him to the narrow path and thought how often they were on gnarled paths stepping through the dark. A damp coolness blew on her ankles as the path opened up to framed black branches with the black water beyond and the liquid dots of light reflected. They stood at the top of a ramp and stars fanned out into a milkier sky and here and there hung luminous clouds in patches and the air was subtle around them and she could see becoming sharper the white of his teeth and his eyes and his shirt. They stood on the sandpaper ramp facing the inner harbor swollen with high tide and the float further out a thin black silhouette with a rowboat overturned on top. He rested his elbows on the railing and bowed his head and she stood beside him with the bone of her ribs against the wood. The sheen in the silk of her dress shone in the dim light like a plant underwater.

It will be different after I tell you, he said. I don't want that.

So don't tell me, she said. She smiled at him sideways, knowing that she shouldn't smile and that this was serious but she was happy and didn't care. Being there with him made her happy and if she was being ridiculous she didn't care. She didn't care if she was absurd.

He was looking awfully grave.

One thing won't change, she said. He looked at her gratefully and stepped behind her and slipped his arms around her front so they faced the same way and she was surrounded by him.

I'd like to stay this way forever, he said.

It cracked. Time came at her like a dart and hit her and something cracked and she knew suddenly that it was a terrible thing he was going to say and already felt the pain of it spread across her chest before knowing what it was.

Tell me.

Maria doesn't have food poisoning.

That wasn't so bad. No? Ann said.

No, it's something else.

Ann's mind spun. *Something else.* Suddenly she didn't know anything. There were hidden things and the panic which follows a lie rose up like a flock of birds and scattered through her. There had been a lie somewhere. Who had lied? Had Harris lied, or Maria? Who had not understood? The vastness of all one did not know rushed at her like the opening of a black tunnel. One minute before she'd been prepared for anything, now suddenly she was struck with how many things could be hidden and how whether she liked it or not those things were going to matter to her and most likely hurt her and she thought with uncharacteristic panic quite possibly destroy her. She braced herself for whoever it was Maria was about to change into. She was about to take on a different meaning. The image appeared to her of Maria lying pale on the bed in the children's house with Harris leaning over her and Maria's hand reaching for his lapel . . .

What? Ann said in a flat voice.

She's having a baby. His voice was small, telling himself. That is, we are. We're having a baby.

And everything did change. The sky sort of jolted to a stop. The stars became negative black dots, the water solid. The trees bristled where they stood but their attitude was changed. Everything switched into something else, something sharper and more clear. Truth had that effect and it seemed this was the most true thing anyone had ever said. The future she'd pictured before her slammed down like a blade and the night parted onto another future, one without her in it, and Harris behind her with his arms still holding onto her was not the same man. He was altogether not the same man. He was a man having a baby with a woman named Maria and Maria was an altogether greater thing than Ann could ever be. Ann was suffocating. His arms were crushing her, she couldn't breathe.

She pushed him off.

She stepped away and held onto the railing. There was no air here either. She needed another harbor to breathe in, she needed another planet.

For a long time neither of them spoke. Finally she managed a word. God, she said.

Night, sky, water. They were all still there. She never wanted to see stars again. She never wanted to see black water at night. She was out of his arms and could never go back into them.

When did you know? she said.

Tonight. She told me.

After the wedding?

Before, he said.

Before the wedding . . . so he knew that afternoon. He knew during the wink in the church. He knew beside her in the tent when he'd been unable to eat.

She found out in Chicago. She wanted to wait before telling me but—

He knew while they were dancing when she thought she'd passed into another dimension. He had not been with her. He was thinking of someone else, of something else. Then it occurred to her that he might be happy. He was going to have a child and he loved Maria. He had said he loved Maria. Maybe he was overjoyed.

Are you glad? she said. She didn't know it was there till she heard it out loud and was surprised to find the hate in her voice.

Ann, he said.

She looked at his face turned away. He was at the end of a long tunnel in the darkness and she could hardly hear him he spoke so softly. It's awful, he said, and a wind came blasting from where he stood and she didn't know which way to face. He was not going to be hers, he belonged to someone else, there was nothing to be done and yet . . . what was she going to do? *That is we are we're having a baby.* At the end of the long tunnel in a howling wind she barely heard, I can't leave her.

No, said Ann. It was just a sound to show she was still there. No. But why ever speak again? What was worth saying? Harris, she thought. She certainly couldn't say my Harris now.

Starkly in an instant she saw herself as she really was—alone in a wood standing among blue shadows with no sounds and the air a sort of black ice. She had no coat. All the people she'd known had forgotten her. Her mother, biting off thread between her teeth, couldn't hear her, and her father with his eyes turned sorrowfully inward did not see her. They never had. Those she loved did not need her. Lila and Carl danced together in a bubble. Ralph Eastman picked lint from his sleeve. Buddy tucked in his shirttails, jumped in a truck and drove away. Fiona Speed showed the back of her hat, heading downtown in a cab. They all had more important concerns, they were all in their own lives, and there was no room for her. At night their doors were shut and through lit windows she could see them consulting one another, checking the baby, looking after business, licking envelopes, turning back the bedcover, shutting off the light switch, while she was left stranded out in the chill night in the true human state, lost, in the dark, alone.

She would not have Harris, she would not have anyone. Harris would have someone. So it was going to be worse for her. She saw now that she would have it worse.

He was saying something, a murmuring was coming from his direction. He was a new person. Did people ever stop changing? They surprised you with fresh pain. Sometimes they surprised you with happiness, but the pain was the sharper surprise. There was no way to protect yourself from it. People could always change and always hurt you. Of course it went in the other direction too, you could hurt them when you didn't intend it and that too was out of your control.

She put down her flag and tried to listen.

He sounded hypnotized. I never pictured it with her, he said. I pictured it with you. He laughed strangely. I didn't even know you, and I pictured having a child with you. He turned toward Ann and looked into her face so she might explain to him this extraordinary thing.

And he appeared again. Harris. He couldn't be, but he was. It was the Harris she'd first seen and his face was suddenly very close and she didn't know if she'd gone to him or he'd come to her but his arms caught her up with a quickness that jolted her heart and set it going wildly. She felt his wet cheek on her face and reached to the tears which had not appeared in his voice and touching them opened doors she'd shut and she felt again a warmth spreading and felt his breath against her ear.

I thought it would be you, he muttered, and a sob disappeared in her hair.

There was nothing to keep in herself. She took his face in her hands and kissed him feeling so near that it was like her face looking out at her own self and her spirit opened wider to him. It could not stop. That's what love was, she thought, throwing open everything and not having it matter if it would go on afterwards. Nothing went on forever. Her bones knew it and her thickened breath knew it and that's what she became. She did not think what anything else meant she simply went out to him unquestioning and immediate and unprotected. He was going away, that was true, that would always be the truth for them, he would always be going but she would not protect herself, she would not withdraw her heart. She left behind negotiation and reason and passed understanding and moved into belief.

He took off his coat, wrapped it around her and lowered her to the ground. She was limp, he paused above her. She drew him down and thought of the rock garden and of swaying against him and of the sail closet lying on his chest and years ago when he had turned around with his sunglasses on at the station holding up her *these yours?* keys and years before that with the salt marshes flickering by and her reflection in the window and she remembered years ago on the boat with the slicing bow how she'd seen another boat on the horizon barely moving with sharp sails and how nothing moved. Her heart was going madly, his mouth was near but did not touch her mouth, his eyes were half-closed.

Look at me, he said.

She thought she'd been to the end of him once but this was further. There was nothing to hold onto but him. She let go of everything and held onto the underside of a cliff with only air around. Her body was being plowed up the middle. It was being split along the sides. Her throat opened up. She let go of hope, there was no more hope. She let go of the future and let go of the memory of all she'd ever lost. It trailed off behind her. None of it mattered. Harris was cupping her chin, Harris pinned her legs.

A dot of light hit his eye.

Is your head alright? he said, and a pine smell came up when he moved his elbows. He held her head. It was like holding the world in his hands, he said. Beneath her were sloping roots and against the sky the outline of a fir tree like black antlers. Something splashed in the water. His head blocked some of the stars. She untucked his shirt and felt the skin of his back, her hands small on his wide back. Your fingers are the same as the air, he said. Each time he touched her in a new place she unraveled more and it was not time anymore but thread, she was a thousand threads and they stretched out and it would never go away. This would stay always, his hair soft as feathers between her fingers, his cheek pressing the hollow of her eye, they would never leave. His hand slid over her throat and tucked into the front of her dress. A tremor went through her. You alright? he said. Oh yes, yes. He took down her strap and smoothed her shoulder and tugged at her clothes pulling them away. She gasped when his mouth found her nipple and he stayed there, flooding her. He worked down the other strap without moving his mouth. Please don't stop, she thought *stay like that always* and she felt exposed to the night till his other hand came over her. He was steering her, she rose to it, she could not get enough of what he was doing to her. Her fingernails dug into the ground. Where was he taking her? She didn't want to know. Who was she? Who cared. She tilted beneath his hips, he moved over her like a mountain. Inside she was crashing like the bottom of a waterfall. His fingers touched her ear then his hand spread out and covered her face.

There was nothing to seal off the world. The black sky did not cover them, it was the opposite of a covering, it drew them up. The sky was an example of how far distance could go. I go on forever, it said, nothing can be contained. She was the same, she went on forever. She felt everything in her. Good and bad were not so different, she inhabited them equally. She was never more herself and yet never so altered *this is what you were made for* his departure was there in each touch and she went toward that departure without reservation or need for proof, she went full-fledged. Every nerve had him running through it, electric for him. Only in another person's arms could this happen.

For a moment they were still. His face against hers was dry with his beard slightly rough. His tongue slipped into her mouth. He found her tongue and sucked at it. A groan came from low in his throat. He lifted her dress and ran his palm down her legs and switched to his knuckles. The dark hulk of his shoulders moved to cradle her hips. His face lay on her stomach. She squeezed her knees against him. His hands slipped under her pulling her underwear inching it down to her ankles. His face tipped down and his tongue was there wet, it slid in the wet opening and silent bright explosions went off in her head flashing down her spine and fizzing

up through her neck into the bones above her eyes and spreading
in a fan. She clutched his collar. His hand came up roaming over
her chest and her chin and her throat. He pried open her mouth
and felt her teeth. He looked at the length of her then rose like a
wave and turned her over. Her dress ripped somewhere, she was
being thrown off balance, her arm flung out. He pushed apart her
knees. One of her shoes was still on and the toe of it dug into the
earth. She stayed very still. He pulled one shoulder back and flattened her on the ground. There was something in her he needed,
he was going after it, his hands were searching for it. She twisted
like hot glass. He flipped her back over and stared down kneeling
above her, something rose from her skin a heat she never knew she
had. She watched him unbuckle his belt. His face had a look she
could not read, he was intent and concentrated and deep in himself, pushing off his pants and struggling to kick them off. In the
soft air she saw the outline of his hip and flank and leg and then
the dark root floating stiff from his silhouette and didn't dare touch
him there right away. His chest came down warm on her warm
skin and she reached down to take hold of him and wrapped her
palm softly around him and he sighed in a new way and she
gripped him more firmly. Her throat seemed thick and crowded
with words but to speak would be to scatter sand. She saw different sorts of light in her head, squares of window light and the
driveway light of fanning headlights, dots of light on swaying masts
and the petal light under an awning, the mint blue light on a
porch, the buttercup light of the tent, clouds lit with cloudlight, his
teeth in the dark. His fingers were inside her like wet clouds. She
grew wider, the outline of his hair in disarray rose again and he
took her hand aside and reached for himself and lowered himself
down pushing against her, shoving gently then finding her and slipping in.

Her legs went up around him. She had not felt empty till now
being filled she saw that everything without him was empty. Her
head stretched from side to side, her breath stopped. In that
instant everything was suspended and complete, there were the

tiniest threads connecting the stars to the tops of the trees to the outline of his ear to the end of her lifted toes. Her head was rolling inside and she shuddered around him and pulled him close.

She was being thrown slowly off a cliff and she made a great arc and didn't drop but stayed up and flew and kept flying and instead of falling could dip down and not hit the ground. His hand was under her lower back, he was moving over her. She had endless capacity, she could go on endlessly, nothing would stop her. This flying would go on forever. His mouth vibrated over her breast, nibbling at her, and when she was gone it would still be there in history, she would be forever unraveling and peeling back for him. He pulled her knee to his chest, he could crush her if he wanted, it would be stamped on her soul. He unfolded her and looked at her body then at her eyes then back over his shoulder at her foot in the air. He was propped up, she was beneath him flying. She flew over fields with animals grazing, over couples embracing, she flew over people shouting and bodies lying lifeless on the ground, past children playing—they stopped and raised curious faces as she passed overhead—she went over crashing rocks and foamy water. His arms were straining holding himself up, elbows locked. He made no sound. He stared down. Her shadow zoomed. It stretched out over the ground then bunched up fat over a bump in a hill then flat again like a dark mat on the speeding water, turned fuzzy-edged and serene over a grassy plain. She could not tell where she stopped. He swooped down, kissed her, pulled up again. She could not tell where . . . her nerves were fluttering, her hands curved around him.

Later her life would be full of things, full of houses and children and trips to the sea and husbands and hats with brims and dogs catching sticks and tables to set and lists to cross off and she would have left singing behind and the stars would never look this way again, they would be further away but at odd unexpected moments something of the stars might strike her and it would be as if someone had branded her forehead with a hot iron. She could not name it, the thing hitting her for an instant, and would not recall what had once been in her head at another time with other stars, but she would have the sense that she'd lost something and not know what it was and not want to find out. She sensed it might be too great to bear.

He poured over her and everything she'd ever learned poured by *I will blame this on the unborn* she thought knowing the meaning was slanted and other tilted phrases drifted by torn *all the past is in these three days* not making sense either. A powder green statue stood in the rock garden, trees were flashing by his profile, she was put in different positions and at the end was supposed to choose one, there were thorns against a green sky, people waving on the pier, a purple eel curled on sand, planes taking off and landing. Her back was bent. Someone was kicking up dust. Her clothes were ripping slowly. *I am scaling the leader* she thought. A hillside of goldenrod shook, a crest of red dune grass blew, *I am arranged for an explosion.* A door slammed shut. Her hair was undone and blowing. Pages flapped. He was moving another way *do you like that? tell me.* On a windowseat lay a woman naked, outside a man was hammering, below in the red library an old man nursed his nurse's breast. There was music playing down the hill, music playing in the other room, stools lined up at a bar. A man sat at the bar and pulled a woman over when she walked by, she was a stranger in tight-fitting clothes, he lifted her skirt and took her from behind pressing her breasts on the counter, his teeth were clenched. His pace changed quickening, she was being rolled over boat hulls half-submerged. He hauled her through fishermen hauling in heavy nets. Lilies were open undisturbed in spreading light. A screen window slit down the middle. He put his hand over her mouth. A tail flicked the water, a mermaid diving down. Lights came on underwater. She was in floodlights on a stage. The audience was all men, row after row of level eyes watching her bare-legged. She moved an ankle, moved an arm, she took off her skirt. They watched her hold it up, studying her. She rose around him, he lifted her. She lay on an airplane wing, the flaps were up, she was tilted, she managed somehow not to fall off *do you know how that feels.* She was being blown, the wind was fierce, she was being strangled, she wanted to be strangled. The woods were shady, a deer stood alert in a clearing. She was tied to a tree, her wrists were tied, the deer was trussed, its hooves bound together. His hand was on her ankle, his hand held her wrists, it held her throat. He threw her onto her back, he threw her off a cliff. She was spread wide, she was soaring tilted like a bird over the unstirred desert with shadows a mile long. The wind howled. Her arms were beating and her wings flapping. The air was vibrating. She was in a yellow cloud and black figures behind the swirl were watching *I will blame this on the unborn.* She strained upward *Harris Harris* clinging upward. She was coming up to a rise. He did not hear her. The men were hammering, the men were watching, the music was playing. He went ahead of her then she caught up and went past ahead of him. She came to the top of the rise. The hills went off in the distance. They kept going and going and going and light was bursting. It burst her apart. She was trampled by light, convulsed in the swirling air. Everything was rippling and she was buried, rippling in waves of light and it fell like yellow dust. It fell around her, dissolving, dissolving, and she dissolved with it falling in dust forever around her falling and falling until it stopped.

# 13. THE PLUNGE

On the north side of Three O'Clock Island were beaches of smooth stones where they used to walk at sunset. On the south side the beaches were shorter flanked by shale rock spotted with pumpkin-colored lichen. The sharp outcroppings grew steeper and more jagged as they moved east to the tip where a cliff jutted out like the prow of a ship. Except for Lost Man's Island which lay like a low slug along the horizon there was nothing between the tip and the Atlantic beyond. At high tide people sometimes jumped into the water. It was called the Plunge.

Ann did not go with them there, but she heard the story so many times their night grew more vivid than her own. She had never described her own night to anyone. She told the fact of it to Lila but not its story. So when Gigi went running back up the grass to Buddy at the truck it was where later Ann went too.

The truck bumped deeply turning onto the grass Promontory road. Buddy drove. Gail Slater beside him held his beer. Ralph

Eastman next to her called out warnings. In the back was Gigi flung against Oliver Granger who'd abandoned Lily who rode back to town with the Cutlers, also Vernon Tobin leaning concerned toward Kingie, and Lizzie Tull passing a whiskey bottle to Carl's friend Monty. Branches would have been scraping the sides and rocks scraping the bottom of the truck. Ralph offered to take the wheel when the truck fishtailed and Buddy said he could drive it blindfolded and switched off the headlights to prove it.

The sky went brighter in the darkness and everyone stared dazzled. Fat stars were clustered in the trees like diamonds. The headlights came back on and lit up a crooked apple tree beside ghostly tall grass and the truck swayed to a stop on the soft field. The engine went off and the night was silent.

They spilled out of the truck, their eyes not adjusted to the dark. They made their way to the shore and followed one another along the narrow path and the night began to take its effect. On one side were sharp branches and dark woods and on the other a thin screen of birch gripping the cliffside and the sound of water lapping below. Oliver Granger turned now and then to take Gigi's hand though her step was more adept than his—she'd been scrambling along this path all her life—and Lizzie hung close to Volentine Montgomery. The only thing I can see is your hair, she said, and when he turned around her face shot forward cobra-like and she kissed him and hurried past laughing. Ralph held a branch for Gail stepping by. Careful, he said. Buddy stumbled over the tree roots. Everyone grabbed onto someone else, moving through the darkness, each after something.

Kingie held Vernon's hand as he led her slowly forward. How steep was the drop to the right? Her eyes were beginning to see. Vernon told her about the man who lived on the Promontory. He howls at the moon, he said.

They came to the narrow outcropping which led to the Plunge and everyone ducked under a fallen tree and came out on the grassy island. Gigi and Oliver dangled their legs over the sheer face and Kingie came onto the prow brushing twigs from her face and brushing at her dress. Then she looked around. Vernon, she said, gazing at the sky. You didn't say it was like this, and she swiveled to her knees. Gail asked Buddy for a cigarette though she never smoked and when he lit the match her face was glowing with adoration.

Gigi stood up. I'm going in.

Ann Lord traveled along the window and down the frame and the curtain swelled out in a deep lung breath. A tablecloth blew up and there were bare legs under the table and she was wearing white underpants. Then she was on her knees *these yours?* Then she remembered stepping inside a door in the dark and being shoved back into the corner where the hinge was and having her skirt jerked up and the suddenness of it taking her breath away and the panting in her ear . . . but who had that been? She remembered her cheeks burning but not which man it was.

Me too, said Gail Slater, and she stepped to the edge. She and Gigi were the same height and their silhouettes would have looked like male and female versions of the same figure, Gigi curved in a waisted dress, Gail with long pants and short hair. Gail undid Gigi's zipper and a hush fell over everyone.

Later Lizzie said that Gigi wasn't drunk really, but just the way she got, loose and running at a high pitch and maybe more intense with this being Lila's wedding night, but a way they'd seen before with an air of disaster about her as if she didn't care if she threw herself away. Ollie Granger was encouraging her mood. Buddy faced the other way, determined to ignore her, swigging his beer.

Gigi slipped off her dress. She was wearing a sort of corset underneath which showed up light against her dark arms. Gail pulled her shirt over her head and stepped out of her pants. Everyone watched them in their underwear looking down. The water swished below. At the same time they removed what they had left on.

There's a rock down there, Buddy said gruffly.

I know. I know where it is. Gigi's voice rose with excitement.

Let's go, Gail said. She took Gigi's hand and they screamed and leapt and disappeared. There was a hollow splash. Everyone stood up, some more steadily than others, and peered over the edge. Splashing and gasping rose from the dull black water below.

*How is it? Freezing! It's great!*

Ollie was already out of his jacket and loosening his tie. Naked he jumped blindly into the air. *Here I come!* He smacked the water like a fist.

O.K. Ralph Eastman said, O.K. and taking off everything but his boxers pinched his nose and flew into the night.

Monty heard a small tree snap behind him and turned to see Buddy thrashing through the bushes off the bluff. He pointed him out to Lizzie. He's just going to get sick, she said.

The dark figures came up over the crest dripping and grabbed their clothes. Gail looked around holding her shirt to her chest. Where's Buddy? Her voice was fresh and expectant.

He's doing a Buddy, Lizzie said.

He left?

When they got back to the truck there was no Buddy. They began calling, lone cries in the orchard. Gigi stood on the truck. Buddy! She laughed, Answer me right now! They knew he might have started to walk home or gone down to the beach to wait and watch the sun rise. One night he had slept under a tarpaulin at WhyKnot boatyard and walked into the kitchen while everyone was having breakfast. So the cries were not insistent.

They loitered in the field for a while and began to show signs of fatigue. It was time to go. Vernon thought they should go and so did Ollie Granger. Only Gail Slater pacing at a distance from the truck, peering into the woods, was not ready to leave.


Teddy came into the living room after being up with her. His arms were folded decisively across his chest. I think she should go to the hospital.

Constance was picking shriveled petals out of a bouquet of freesia. She hated it at the hospital.

Teddy sat on an armrest. No one sat in normal places anymore. She is not in good shape, he said.

No, Constance said. She's got cancer. Constance who usually took care with her clothes was wearing the same pants and shirt she'd had on for three days.

Margie lay sprawled on the floor, her head leaning back against a Turkish hassock, her expression uncertain. An air of uncertainty had pretty much taken over the house.

She's just so bad . . . said Teddy. His arms dropped to his sides.

That breathing, Margie said.

You mean the rattling, Constance said.

So awful.

What do you think exactly hurts her? Nina said, coming in. She carried a large bottle of Evian which she drank from in deep swigs.

Everything, Teddy said.

But is it, I don't know, a stabbing pain or nausea or like a migraine?

Jesus, Nina, Constance said.

Probably all of that alternating, Margie said. Plus more.

Weird we don't dare ask her, Nina said. It's not as if she's not thinking about it.

She probably tries not to think about it. Constance piled the brown petals in one palm.

Nausea is the worst, Nina said.

They're all pretty bad. Teddy stared at the floor. It's hard to watch.

Imagine how it is for her, Nina said.

That's what I mean.

Constance crushed her handful of brown petals and left the room to throw them away. Margie glanced up and saw Teddy's shoulders shaking in little downward shrugs and watched Nina walk over to him and put her hand on his back. It's O.K., she said. Behind them the afternoon light lit up the ivy. It's O.K.

Teddy turned his face to her, his eyes brimming. Is it? he said sharply. I don't think so, I don't think it's O.K. at all.

Nina's hand sprang back as if she'd touched a hot iron. His expression suddenly changed—he didn't mean it. He tried to take back her hand but she'd turned and moved away out of his reach.


They began to climb back into the truck. Ralph Eastman slipped unquestioned into the driver's seat and everyone else took the same places like children at assigned desks.

Gail was the last to step up on the running board. So we're just going to leave him? she said, and she pulled shut the door.

Ralph started the engine and flicked on the lights and waited for everyone to settle down in the back, frowning through the cab window. He wasn't going to drive with anyone standing up. He pressed the brakes, lighting up the grass behind them red, and started to back up. The field was full of lumps and the truck tilted and there were squeals as everyone was thrown more against each other. Ralph cranked the wheel and drove forward a little then backed up again this time over a steeper bump making them all laugh. Gigi swung up to the driver's window with Ollie holding her waist to tease Ralph and after passing over one mound the truck suddenly gunned back jolting everyone and the front wheels humped up and Gigi was laughing, banging on the side door and Ralph, irritated, kept looking back over his shoulder to steer.

Gail screamed.

It was not a playful scream and everyone in the back went silent. Gail's arm came chopping down onto Ralph and the truck jerked to a stop and her door flew open and she ran forward stumbling over the grass lit up behind by the headlights.

It's Buddy, she cried.

No one understood. They sat up in the back and saw Gail pounce onto the ground. Then they saw the white shirt of the figure in the grass. Her face turned back furious at the blinding headlights. She screamed back to the truck. If she'd had time to think Gail Slater would not have said what she did. Gail Slater was a quiet person, the sort of person who did the dishes without being asked and took the seat no one else wanted, who did not judge others, a person who would not have deliberately given Ralph Eastman less reasons for happiness in his life, and therefore would not have said what she could not afterwards take back, a cry in a moment of shock. Ralph opened the door to come help and Gail Slater screamed at him, Look what you did!

Panic swept through the back of the truck and everyone scrambled up and ran toward Gail and the unmoving figure on the ground. Buddy lay on his back with his head bent unnaturally to the side and his glasses crumpled near his ear. Lizzie said she noticed one eye partly open and Vernon said he saw it too, an eye picking up the headlight's beam.

Don't move him, Oliver Granger said. He might have broken his back.

Gigi lowered herself as if drawn to the ground by a magnet. Buddy, she said. Bud. Her wet hair fell on his shoulder.

What are we going to do? Lizzie said impatiently.

Gail lifted her hand into the light and they saw dark blood on it. Move back.

It's his head. His ear's bleeding.

We should get a doctor before we move him.

Harris. Someone should get Harris.

Ralph took off his jacket and he and Gail lay the jacket over Buddy's chest.

The Thornes', Gail said.

I don't think they're here.

They've got a phone.

Buddy, Gigi whispered. Buddy. She started to cry.

Come on, Gail said.

This is bad, Lizzie said. This is really bad.

We should not move him, Oliver said.

I'm going to the Thornes', Vernon said. He touched Kingie's shoulder. I'll be right back. He ran up the road and disappeared in the dark.

Gail was crouched by his head. He's still breathing.

Of course he's still breathing, snapped Gigi.

He was under the car, Ralph said softly. How could we not've seen him?

It can't be good for him in this wet grass.

He shouldn't be moved.

Lizzie turned to Oliver. Would you like to say that a fifth time?

Do you think his neck is broken?

God.

How far is the Thornes'?

I think the wheel ran over his head, Gail said.

Buddy, can you hear me? Gigi said. Buddy. She put her ear to his mouth and waited. Then she looked up at everyone around her lit with shadows and found no help there and went back close to him, weeping. You're going to be alright, she said. Buddy. We're all here and you're going to be alright.

A rope dropped out of the sky. She held onto it and was pulled up into the clouds. She arrived at a car dealership. It was deserted with no salesman on the lot. She wandered back to the garage which was like her father's leather factory and way in the back found the entrance to a cave. She walked into it and in the middle of a long dark passageway came upon a white sliver of sole, a glowing fillet of fish lying on the ground. She bent to touch it and was knocked backwards by a man in black armor wearing the helmet of a beetle. His backhand knocked her to the ground.

Vernon Tobin arrived at the Thornes' dark house and tried the doors on the porch, then picked up a stone and rapped on a pane till the glass shattered. He reached past the sharp edges and unlocked the tab on the inside latch and let himself in. He saw the dim shape of a tulip light and pulled the beaded cord and found himself in an unpainted wooden hallway with low ceilings. He went through to the kitchen and tugged the buoy hanging from a string and that light went on and he saw a large clock on the wall with its red second hand gliding. Ten past three. The kitchen was yellow and under a yellow hutch he saw a black phone. He picked up the receiver. Come on, he said out loud, come on.

After a while a woman's voice answered. What number please.

Is that Shirley? Vernon said.

No Shirley's off tonight. The operator spoke slowly and normally and the normality of it nearly made Vernon weep. This is Ruthie.

Hi, he burst out. This is Vernon Tobin. There's been a—it's an emergency.

Tell me the emergency, Vernon, said Ruthie in a calm voice.

Vernon told her. Telling it made him feel faint. He took a deep breath.

Where are you calling from? Ruthie said.

I had to break into the Thornes' because they're not here, but everyone's still down on the Promontory, you know in the field where you park . . .

I do. Now Vernon. I'm going to call Foy Hopkins and tell him and he'll be right down.

And a doctor, Vernon said. He needs a doctor.

I'll tell Foy. You wait at Thornes' and I'll call you back. Alright?

Vernon nodded and hung up the phone.

Each year there was a different doctor who came and lived in the doctor's house. There'd been the young doctor with the wife and children, and a chubby one who halfway through August had a heart attack. There was the one who drank a lot who diagnosed Mrs. Ellis as having a spider bite when she really had shingles. The summer doctor was not the most reliable. Then Vernon thought of Harris Arden. He had not liked Harris Arden when he watched him dance with Ann Grant but now he felt Harris Arden was a friend and wished that he were there.

The clock was at nearly three-twenty. He saw his reflection in the glass panes of the cabinet with the plates and cups behind and wished he were still with everyone else down at the field. He felt both hollow and jazzed up. Buddy would be O.K. he told himself.

He had to be. He recalled the strange twist of his head in the tufted grass and when he thought of that it was hard to keep believing he would be O.K. Vernon's chest ached.

He'd been in this kitchen before at the Thornes'. Andy Thorne was someone he used to play with a long time ago, they used to play war games when they were young. The best part was capturing Andy's sister Carol. But Andy Thorne had been in and out of institutions the last ten years and the last time Vernon had seen him was on the ferry a few summers ago. Andy had put on a lot of weight though his voice was still the same. Who knew where Andy Thorne was now. Vernon knocked against the enamel stove and it shook. *Royal Rose* it said on the back. He kept thinking of the sliver he could see of Buddy's eye and the way his head was pressed too close to his shoulder. It didn't look like Buddy. He walked quickly into the front hall and looked down the road which was silent and dark. Glass crunched under his feet but he wasn't going to pick the glass up. His heart was going fast and light. The phone rang. He ran back to it.

Vernon, Ruthie. Foy Hopkins is on his way. He'll be there at Thornes' to pick you up and you can take him down to Buddy Wittenborn.

O.K.

You O.K. then, said Ruthie very calm.

A shaky voice responded that he was. He thanked her.

You're welcome, Ruthie said. Now. Should you let Buddy's mother and father know?

Oh. I guess so. I guess I should.

That might be a good idea, Ruthie said. I'll connect you. Now I have three numbers here for Wittenborn.

Four-seven-three-oh is the main house.

One minute.

The phone started to ring. It rang many times. In the middle of a ring a voice surprised Vernon. You sure they're home? Ruthie said on the line.

Yes.

The ringing stopped. Hello?

Who's this? Vernon said.

Who's *this?*

Aunt Linda, it's Vernon.

Christ Vernon. What are you kids doing?

He told her what had happened.

Dick! she screamed into the phone. Then, Where are they? Dick! Where are you?

Vernon told her and told her Foy Hopkins was on his way.

Dick! she screamed into the receiver. It's the kids! Now wait tell me what happened.

Vernon told her again and realized with dread that this was not the last time he would have to tell this story, he would probably be telling this story all his life. Dick! she kept shouting. Dick!

Then Vernon heard footsteps in the background and a voice and his Aunt Linda saying, Buddy has run over someone at the Promontory.

No, Vernon said. Buddy's the one hurt.

I don't think she heard that, came Ruthie's voice still on the line.

I'm trying to—Aunt Linda was speaking away from the receiver. Stop talking to me and I'll find out.

Then Dick Wittenborn's voice was on the phone, stern and deep. Vernon, he said, now what is all this about?

# 14. WAKE UP PARIS

She was underwater and had to walk carefully to stay on the bottom. The walls of the pool were robin's-egg blue and she held a white lily. A man laughed and bubbles came out. He had once been her lover. When they hauled him out upside down his white shirt was plastered to his skin.

In the palm of her hand was the tiniest bird she'd ever seen.

The summer streets of Beacon Hill were empty. They arrived at the end of the day. She didn't remember the flight from the island or the drive from the airport into town. She remembered being in the room upstairs, she remembered it dimly. The house was dim and the halls dark and everything was covered in sheets and there were no signs of life. The Grangers had many spare bedrooms since they had no children and Oscar agreed with Oliver Granger that Ann should not be left alone. Ollie's figure filled the doorway with the dark hall behind. Everything alright? he said. She could not feel anything she recognized having felt before. This was a new pain she'd not known and when she didn't answer he came forward and said, Ann I don't know what to say and sat on the bed. She had stopped being someone named Ann and was hardly a woman any-more, she was only a mother and also not a mother as she had been and it was too hard to explain anything and easier instead to sink against his arm when his arm came around her. He was solid and his body was warm. She could not speak to say no, she didn't move away or toward him, she was not thinking no, she was not thinking yes, she was not thinking anything. They were waiting for the body, that's what they were doing. Oscar had gone down to Virginia after Ollie had flown them back in his plane and she was at the Grangers' on Beacon Hill waiting. Her blank eyes stared into the back of her head at nothing and his arms in a cotton shirt were around her pressing and easing her back onto the bed. She looked up at the ceiling and noticed a decorative trim of crimson grapes at the top of the walls and thought how Lily must have put it up. It's alright, he said. It's good for you to cry. She shielded her eyes with her arm and he might have thought the light was too bright, he reached across her chest and turned out the lamp and the room was so dark she couldn't see anything. The shades were down and the shutters closed and with no light anywhere it was like being sealed in a crypt. He was big and heavy on her and she could not see him. His mouth found hers wet, her whole face was wet. It was like being underwater at night. She felt him like water. Strange how a thing felt so dimly as those strange arms around her in the middle of disorienting grief should have the consequences it did, while another thing in another time and another darkness which had meant so much to her which had in fact meant everything would never show anything of itself in the world. It might just as well not have happened for all it showed. That greater thing disap-peared and never took on a life of its own. While out of this other darkness, this other evening in July some fifteen years later, another life did come despite the lack of shared sentiment, a life unquestioned by the man whose name she shared, who believed himself the father, a life which was now at that moment a young woman beneath Ann Lord making notes in the margins of her play-book about street kids in Brooklyn, sitting on a chaise in the back garden at the shaded end of the lawn.

They lay on his coat on the moss and she felt the sticks and roots which she had not felt before as he was crashing over her. The grass by her cheek was the same as her cheek and the same as the air and all of it was part of the universe and his hand by her chin and his face curved on her neck was part of it too.

Maybe I will after all.

What?

Have your baby.

He pulled her closer. I'd love that, he said. They could say any-thing now.

Might not be so simple, she said.

No.

With you married to someone else.

It would be ours, he said. That's how bad I am, I would like it.

But you would stay with her.

He didn't answer. She still had the conviction of his hands on her and did not yet feel the misery which she knew was coming. Mis-ery was just outside the circle around them, waiting in the dark-ness. They held each other and his weight was more real than his going away.

There were things she'd not asked him and things she'd not said and she did not wonder what she knew or what she had learned but merely felt what had happened and felt what it meant. She did not need to explain it, she simply had it. He was asleep in her arms and the stars which had been spilling and spilling had stopped and were motionless and she knew that what they'd had was not enough but believed it would have to be.

Then the white ceiling opened like an eye and she saw what the ceiling might have seen, how she'd never put words to it.

All her life she'd listened to talk, life was full of talk. People said things, true and interesting things and ridiculous things. Her father used to say they talked too much. There was much to say, she had said her share. How else was one to know a thing except by naming it? But words now fell so far from where life was. Words fell on a distant shore. It turned out there were other tracks on which life registered where things weren't acknowledged with words or given attention to or commented on. It might have been said, These two had a story. One might have said she'd found in him the great thing, that she'd found more than herself which was everything and found more than life. And even saying that she would not bring back what was gone. She did not know if it had been the same for him. She would never know. She only knew for herself. Nowhere did it show. Without being shared, what they knew had faded into a kind of mirage. It became One of Those Things. She could not let what passed between them matter too much afterwards so that when the memory tried to assert itself it had been pushed down by reason and habit and time, eventually becoming no more than a scruffy hidden scar on a scruffy hillside. She had worked to rub it out. That this had been forgotten once and would be forgotten again suddenly seemed worse to her than her own life ending.

The sisters huddled near the door.

Completely out of it, Margie said, shaking her head.

Nina's eyes narrowed. What's she saying?

Have you sold the cathedral yet?

They laughed quietly.

Constance studied Margie's face. What else?

You know, Leave the dishes . . . oh this one's good: Wake up Paris.

Paris? Constance said.

No, Nina said. Harris. She's saying Harris. She was saying his name before.

Harris?

Who's Harris?

An exchange of glances made it clear no one knew.

Maybe Aunt Grace . . . Margie said.

They stared at their mother.

Let's ask *her,* Nina whispered. She nudged Margie and they crept toward the bed.

Mother? Constance said.

The eyes blinked feebly.

Mother.

Present.

The girls smiled.

Who is Harris? Constance leaned closer.

Harris. Ann Lord's eyes opened a crack. She didn't see them.

Yes Harris. Who is he?

Their mother began to smile as if hearing the answer to a riddle. She nodded. Harris, she said.

Yes. Harris. Constance got easily exasperated. Who is Harris?

Harris, Ann Lord took a deep breath as if starting to tell a story. Harris was . . .

The girls stayed very still. Their mother's low-lidded gaze was directed out the window. He was . . . she said, and her gaze suddenly turned and regarded her daughters with eyes not drugged in the least. Harris was me.


He slept in her arms and she wondered about bracing herself for how it was going to be without his weight on her but couldn't imagine it and stopped trying. *I am with him now.*

She did not tell him then or ever how she felt.

Out of the night she heard someone shouting. *Harris! Harris!* It was Gigi wanting to play another game, Gigi with her whims and desires whirling around at this late hour. Harris lay breathing deeply on her, smooth-eyed, and didn't hear and Ann Grant was not going to wake him.

* * *

Her collarbones shivered as she took a breath. Did anything come after that? she said.

Your life. You had a life after that.

Is that what it was.

Yes. A full life, a family. Apparently a few families. He laughed. And you saw the world. . . .

Some of it.

And husbands. You had a few of those.

I had them and I lost them. I lost— She stopped herself. One should not have to live through some things. You said that once I remember.

Did I?

Yes about the war. We were on the sailboat.

I remember the sailboat.

And your family? she said. What children?

Four. Three girls and a boy.

It was happy?

Happy enough.

I would have wanted better for you than happy enough.

Happy enough is fine with me.

You must think me spoiled, she said. I'm not you know.

We can't help what we want. Only how we act when we don't get it. Or do.

You think me spoiled.

Not spoiled. Maybe a little hard. Maybe life has made you a little hard.

She thought for a moment. What has it made you?

Soft. He laughed.

I could have made you more than happy enough, she said.

Maybe. It's an easy thing to say.

Well that's me, she said. Easy and hard.

He shook his head. I don't believe in regret. Things turn out the way they do for a reason.

And is reason good?

It's the order of things, isn't it?

Order . . . she said softly and softly guffawed. She had learned a few things by now.

✻    ✻    ✻

Gigi looked all over for Harris. She rapped on the windowpane where Maria di Corcia slept waking her and not finding him turned on her heel and ran back toward the headlights shining on the front porch where dark figures crossed back and forth. Maria must have wondered where Harris was and why they wanted him and what the dark stain was on Gigi's dress but none of them were people she knew and after looking toward the house and spying Lizzie Tull coming out the front door with an armload of jackets and Ralph Eastman getting in the station wagon, she probably went back to bed.

Gigi burst through the cottage door. The lights were on, no one there. Harris! she screamed. Ralph and Lizzie pulled up in the idling car outside.

*Harris!*

It was the scream Ann Grant heard through the trees. It echoed the name going through her head. It was the scream she ignored.

There was no way of knowing if it would have made a difference if Buddy had gotten treatment sooner or if Harris Arden's particular knowledge of head injuries from the war would have helped. They were to go over many times the events of that night and when Harris was asked where he'd been he said simply he was taking a walk with Ann Grant so that when Ann heard it the next morning from Lizzie she was struck by the smoothness of his saying they were together without saying exactly how and not having it be a lie and was grateful for his answer though it left her more heavily with what only she knew—that she had heard Harris being called and had not woken him and had not answered.

Each person thought of what he or she might have done that night, that Gail Slater might have stayed at Buddy's side where she preferred to be instead of jumping off a cliff to impress him or that Monty could have followed Buddy into the brush if he'd done what he wanted and slipped away from Lizzie Tull resting heavily on his thigh, that Lizzie if less fixated on Volentine Montgomery might not have stopped where Monty stopped at the back fender but stepped forward to see Buddy's leg, or Kingie herself having a father who disappeared at parties to turn up later after napping in the garden or on a back porch had instead of dangling her legs at the back of the truck smoking a cigarette leaned forward a little to the right and seen Buddy slumped by the wheel or Gigi who might not have led them to the Promontory in the first place and brought them instead to canoe at Phinns Pond or climb Carrie's Peak or gone to the graveyard near the Grange or done any of the other things they'd done other nights. They might not even have left the house at all and drifted up to the porch and let the night dwindle as they had many other summer nights half-noticing shooting stars, sneaking the Wittenborns' liquor. Then Buddy would still be there, adjusting his glasses, sleeping through breakfast, coming in the door with a bucket of clams, Buddy with a bag unzipped going back to college in September, needing a haircut, forgetting his keys, who would play hockey and kiss girls and see snow falling and get married, wake to rain, go grey.

And finally there was Ralph Eastman who may have thought of a thousand things he might have done differently but did not need to think past the first one. He might not have backed up the truck, he might simply have driven forward.


A hand rose up from the bed. Nora, she said.

The padding was a tired white then it turned yellow like tea roses then something went wrong and acid green was burning through, leaking pain. More padding! She needed more padding. Nurse Brown rubbed the needle.

Do you ever wonder what you'd be like if you never . . . Ann Lord's voice trailed off.

Never what?

Never met up with the people in the attic.

After the injection she lay herself alongside a man in a Chinese junk. He was wearing wrinkled clothes and she was naked against him with the wooden ribs of the boat like a cradle and the river flat in the grey dawn. The way he held onto her made her believe he loved her and the way he looked at her made her think he would never let her go.

After the scream Ann heard a car driving on the dirt road and saw its headlights lighting up the bridge. Then she fell asleep. She woke to the sound of a car coming back up the driveway. Harris' hair was against her face, he was heavy on her.

He jumped a little in his sleep. His head lifted. His eyes opened. He saw nothing then he saw her. He put his arms around her and wrapped them tighter. She thought he would squeeze the breath out of her and wished he would.

They stood up. He brushed the pine needles from his knees and she thought how she hardly knew this person and wasn't it strange she was here with him in the dark zipping up her dress and finding the white glow of her underpants to step into. Then he handed her a shoe and clicked his tongue and snapped back into the person she knew.

They walked up the dark path they would never walk again. Each step they took was away from being together. She saw that now. At the time she did not really believe what she knew was fact, that this was the last time. She still had the reassurance of his body and it threw its cloak over them as they walked. In the dark he took her hand.

✳

Buddy Wittenborn lay on an army cot in the back of the Witten-borns' truck. Foy Hopkins had borrowed the cot from his brother-in-law Chuck Crockett and his sister Phyllis had lent a quilt. Pete Shields had been roused from bed to start up the ferry and as the engine warmed, the Wittenborns' truck was driven down the ramp onto the empty boat. The cot was lifted off the truck by Vernon Tobin and Oliver Granger on one side and Foy Hopkins and Mr. Wittenborn on the other and carried into the passenger cabin with the green leatherette seats and portholes and set unsteadily down in the aisle by the vibrating wall. Dick Wittenborn tripped on the raised threshold stepping out and Foy Hopkins caught his arm from behind. As Ann Grant moved her arm which had fallen asleep under Harris Arden's shoulder the ferry pulled out of the harbor with its lights on in the dark blue morning and Dick Wit-tenborn stood in the windy stern by the coiled rope wiping his eyes. From the landing Oliver Granger and Gail Slater could see the figure of Vernon Tobin climbing the iron steps to the captain's station. Inside Pete Shields answered questions about navigation and talked about radar and about some of the storms he'd seen in his twenty years as captain and he and Vernon had a pleasant con-versation not once mentioning the boy lying beneath them with the women standing over him or a little apart the doctor they'd fetched from the doctor's house who stood by like an uninvited guest looking as if he were about seventeen years old.

The unshakable certainty she had walking up the slant of hill toward the cottage with the lights still on was not something she would ever feel again. Certainty after that had cracks in it.

The compound was deserted.

He followed her into the little kitchen with the yellow ruffled curtains. His necktie was bunched in one hand and he stuffed it into his pocket. He pulled out a chair and sat. Ann took the other chair and he dragged it over across the floor with her in it and lifted her arm and placed her hand on the green checked oilcloth of the table and covered it with his hands looking at it not at her face. He pulled her onto his lap. The sky through the high trees was beginning to lighten. She switched off the lamp on the table and they sat in a bluish light.

So this is the room where we say good-bye, he said.

She got out of his lap and sat in a chair.

He started to talk. She was beautiful, she was going to be fine, anyone who could swim in water that cold would be fine, he wasn't going to worry about her. He smiled. She tried to smile, but couldn't. Her conviction was beginning to break up into little pieces, and she no longer felt like smiling. There was no one like her, she was strong, he only wished he were as strong as she but he wasn't. He looked down. Maria—

Then it broke apart. He said her name and it broke apart. Maria had been there for as long as he could remember, he could not picture life without Maria. Maria knew him and Maria loved him and in his way he loved Maria. Ann Grant watched his mouth and the words coming out, not wanting to hear anymore but not able to stop him. *Maria Maria* it kept coming out of his mouth. Maria looks after me, he said. I need to be looked after.

Ann took her hand out of his. Dark ink was bleeding into the clear water around her. Outside it was still as church, nearly dawn. It seemed as if it had always been nearly dawn.

A bird sang a thin note.

His eyes were pale with the whites showing up. She listened to him but pictured other things. She pictured him driving in a car with his wife beside him, she saw them sleeping together in a bed. She saw other women whose hands he'd take, whose shirts he'd pull off at the shoulder, and other women to whom he would with a sad face say good-bye. She thought of how he'd said, Look at me.

They had been through a lot together, he and Maria. Maria was a part of his family . . .

Ann Grant stared at his hands which sat curved on their sides on the green oilcloth.

I couldn't leave Maria—

No, she said. You couldn't.

She noticed his blue oval cuff links not fastening his cuffs and thought I will never remove those from his sleeve and put them in some little box and she thought of the silver box with the raised red enamel insignia which her father kept on his bureau with his cuff links and collar splints inside.

It's late, he said. You look tired.

She had never been less tired.

I'm going to have to go, he said.

She stared down.

I don't want to, I have to. He didn't move. Will I hear from you?

She looked at him.

No, I suppose not, he said. No I don't see how it would be . . .

They sat in silence. There was the copper sink and the ruffled curtains and the sheen on the green oilcloth. She took his hand. Inside was a voice saying *don't leave don't leave don't leave*

I'll always be with you, he said.

She nodded.

You'll always have the best of me. He squeezed her arm, insisting.

It was as if someone had whacked her on the back. No, she said. She grabbed his shoulders. This is the best of you. And this and this. This is the best of you and what I won't have.

He held her shaking back, leaning awkwardly in his chair. Her face was smashed against his arm and through the space by his elbow she saw the corner of the table and the folded oilcloth with a nail in it and tried to catch her breath. *I can't,* she thought. *I can't. I can't. I can't.*


There was breath still coming from the body lying there. The room was loud and shaking.

This vibrating can't be good for him, said Mrs. Wittenborn. She was careful to blow her cigarette smoke away from Buddy's face. She was wearing an old canvas coat which Lizzie Tull had grabbed

from its rusty hook behind the back hall curtain and she was holding Buddy's hand. The coat was one Buddy used to wear. Out the
window grey water moved slowly by. The lights on the far shore did
not change and the sea seemed to roll in place beneath the flat
hull. The ferry had never been so slow.

❖   ❖   ❖

You wanted to stay didn't you?
   I did.
   I knew it.
   Of course I wanted to stay.
   Actually I didn't know it, I just hoped it.
   I had to go, he said.
   Did you go back to her after?
   When I left you?
   I always wondered.
   Not after you, he said.
   No? Her eyebrows rose. Well at least not right away.

❖   ❖   ❖

He stood outside the door. Who knows what will happen, he said.
   Don't say that.
   You're right, he said. I'm sorry.
   Don't say that.
   I didn't say anything, Mother. I'm just sitting here.
   Her daughter's straight hair came down on either side of her
face.
   Why aren't you in school? A hill came rolling at her.
   I'm not *in* school. Anyway it's July.
   There were dark green footprints on the hill. She must have
gone on after that. She stood at the kitchen door and the grass
turned silver from the sky. She must have gone on.
   I'm acting now. I'm in a play.

That's right, I knew that. Out of the hill came wheels spinning which began to shoot out bits of steel in little darts. She cried out.

God are you O.K.? Nina stood up. Can I get you something?

Her mother's eyes were pressed shut. They opened. A bullet, she said.


Harris Arden came up around the side of the house. He was not used to so much emotion. It wore him out. This had all caught him off guard. He'd come upon a new road and had taken a few steps down that road and now he saw it wasn't the road he was going to take after all. He was going back to the road he knew and would continue walking where he'd been walking for a long time. He'd been walking on that road for a long time for a reason. It suited him, didn't it? Well there wasn't any use in asking whether it suited him or not, it was where his duty took him and where his life had put him and where he would go.

He smelled his sleeve, that was her. She was like a flash of light, surprising him. It had been too sudden. But hadn't it been sudden with Maria also? Why, it could go on being sudden with girls if you let it, one had to put a stop to it somewhere along the line. Having a baby would put a stop to it. Maria was the one he would stop with. And Maria loved him, that was certain. He could not be certain about this new woman. After the brightness faded who knew what would happen, he hardly knew her.

He stepped onto the long porch with dew soaked shoes. Some dim lamps were lit inside. He was surprised to see people still up. Through the window he would have seen Carl's friend Monty bent toward Vernon Tobin's girlfriend Kingie. They were holding cups of tea and looking solemn. He didn't want to disturb them and didn't want to see anyone anyway so he stepped back off the porch and walked back the way he'd come past the garbage cans where the cake boxes were stacked in the blue light.

On the driveway standing near a car was the man in the white dinner jacket whose name he couldn't remember and the tall girl

Gail. When she saw Harris she came running toward him with an
air of panic and it reminded him of overseas and for a moment
thought something had happened to Maria. Gail pulled him into
the car and the man in the dinner jacket got behind the wheel and
before he knew it he was being driven away, needed someplace
else.

The Bishops Harbor public landing was a flimsy dock the size of
a foyer and Clint Stone was there waiting in the *Happenstance* to
bring Harris to the mainland and to Buddy. Maybe they'd beat the
ferry. Clint Stone's wife sat on the stool beside him, a kerchief
under her chin, a thermos in her lap, looking toward the bay. Harris stepped into the boat still in his dark suit, in his pocket he felt
his bunched-up tie. His footfall rang hollow on the floor. The man
in the white dinner jacket untied the painter and Gail held the boat
steady with one foot and for a moment Harris thought she was
going to jump on but instead she gave the boat an angry shove and
stepped back folding her arms over her chest looking suddenly
sixty years old instead of twenty.

Harris Arden turned up his collar as they motored out. He
remembered other louder dawns full of chaos and smoke and
things burning and what it felt like stepping out of the closeness of
a tent. He did not want to think of things which did no good. He
turned his mind from that. Then Ann Grant's face flashed up looking at him sidewise smiling the way she had, standing at the railing
in the dark, and he thought of the curve of her back and her head
turned and her neck and her eyes opening slightly as she lay on her
back and as spray misted his face he had to turn his mind from that,
too. He must not think about that anymore. He frowned and
steered his thoughts toward Maria and the smooth face he knew
well. She was sleeping now, and he thought of how she'd wept a little when he'd checked on her earlier and how he'd told her everything would be fine and how grateful her face had been. Then he
remembered the weeping of the other one and how he could not
reassure her. Well there was only so much a person could do.

✿

I would want it stopped, Nina said.

Well you're not her, Teddy said.

What about what she said?

What?

I'd rather retire.

When did she say that?

The other day. I told you that.

You didn't tell me. I would have remembered.

Aunt Grace came in following her dog and they were silent for a moment.

Oh, Aunt Grace, Constance said. D'you know anyone named Harris, someone Mother knew?

Aunt Grace pulled in her chin thinking. She shook her head. Then she remembered something. We had a cousin named Harry.

Who was he? Margie said eagerly.

Bit of a pansy. Sweet man.

Did Mother know him?

She must have met him. Why what's she saying?

That he pulled her off a garden wall or something.

Margie and Nina laughed.

That doesn't sound like cousin Harry, said Aunt Grace.

Or like Mother, Constance said.


The surface of the water was torn up and navy blue. She was out on the water when the news came about Paul. It was years later, it was years ago. *Is there a Mr. and Mrs. Lord on board?*

The girls must have burned down the house, Oscar had chuckled. Ann was below cleaning up the lunch dishes and heard the sails flapping and felt the boat stop, headed into the wind. She came up the steps into the bright cockpit and saw at the stern the Coast Guard boat and thought they were being checked for life preservers. The captain wearing a yellow slicker held the railing and was talking to Oscar and Matt Hallowell both of whom looked disturbed listening. When Oscar glanced back at her his face was frightened. He signaled to her to come forward, keeping his arm out as he turned back to listen, the arm suspended out as she clutched her way past the ladies' legs, sensing something terrible in the way they watched, hair blowing in her eyes, the boat rising and falling with the swell. When she got near she heard *injury to the head* and Oscar turned and held her arm tightly and looked at her mouth not at her eyes. He said, It's Paul. She turned to the Coast Guard man. What? she said. An accident, he said. Who was he anyway and why was he telling them this and how did he know and what was it? A Mrs. Abbott had contacted them . . . Ann looked at Oscar. It was instantaneous, Oscar said. A boat overturned on the river . . . his face was not equipped for this, he was shaking his head. When did this happen? Ann turned to the Coast Guard man bobbing up and down. We received a call this morning from a Mrs. Abbott, it happened yesterday evening and they reached her this morning in Cambridge from the camp apparently . . . Ann's mind broke into pieces. Yesterday, she thought. Yesterday she'd gone swimming at dusk in a dark green cove where they'd anchored, the second night of their cruise, she'd eaten cheese on a cracker as the sun set, had he still been alive then? As she ate blueberries for dessert he was not, as she slept in the rocking boat he was not . . . she thought she would faint, the sails were flapping madly. The Coast Guard man below her was young with his slicker well worn and cracked and his voice was thin under the flapping and the wind when Oscar asked him, Did you speak with Mrs. Abbott? No, sir, he said. It wasn't me. My wife took the message. Paul was at camp in Virginia where they did take canoes on rivers and Abbott was there in the house in Cambridge to receive the call. All that fit, but Paul was barely twelve and that this had happened did not fit. It did not fit at all.

# 15. SWIM OF THE SECOND HEART

Her forehead was pressed to the door frame. Now it begins, she thought. She stood there a long time. There was a noise outside and hope flared up—he was coming back—then she realized it was a door slamming up at the house.

She turned and went into the bedroom. She crossed the room and stood in a place she'd never stood before in the corner where probably no one had ever stood and pressed herself against the wall and closed her eyes. She remembered how he'd felt and it was like a stab into her and she sank into a heap. She began to sob and the sobbing grew in force till she thought her spine would snap and it went on she couldn't tell how long. When it subsided she stared dumbly like an animal in shock. Her body felt numb and throbbed dully. Scattered around the room she saw things from long ago, the wedding. The green bridesmaid jacket hooked under a light fixture, nylons tangled in a chair, her jewelry pouch unzipped on the bureau. She heard a car and looked out dazed over the sill and recognized the red taillights of Ollie Granger's car. So, they were finally calling it an evening.

A body can have no peripheral pulse and still be alive.

It was loud and shaking in the room.

Can this vibrating be very good? Mrs. Wittenborn said. And still no one answered. She held Buddy's hand and still blew smoke back over her shoulder. Out the windows the horizon was constant. The lights on shore did not change.

The doctor stood above him, stethoscope in his ears, frowning as if determined to look serious. His quiet manner did not inspire confidence. He did not meet anyone's eye. The brace he'd fashioned for Buddy's neck out of knee braces had slipped down and didn't appear to be doing any good. Then Buddy's lips moved. The stern lines on the doctor's boyish face went slack and he leaned down.

What is he saying? Mrs. Wittenborn stood up and stepped back to give him room.

The doctor pressed his fingers on Buddy's throat and listened with the stethoscope to Buddy's chest. Everyone watched except for Vernon Tobin who was sitting with his back to them, staring out the salt-blurred window.

Did he say something? Mrs. Wittenborn's voice had a hysterical edge.

The doctor folded his stethoscope and looked at her blankly. He shook his head.

He was pacing outside on the lawn. A squirrel twitched, a blur in the flower beds. Soon she will be gone, he thought. Soon it will seem as if she is somewhere else, but she won't be anywhere.

Teddy repeated these thoughts in order to make them real. Above him out of the quiet he heard a groan of pain. It came through the open window. The sound was otherworldly and deep and yet more real than anything around him. His heart stood still. He wondered for one panicked moment if it would beat on. It seemed it could not, then it did, it beat on. But he was rattled by the sound—to think that such a sound had come from his mother . . .

Through the French doors he saw the figure of his wife hurrying toward him, waving at him to come inside. She was without the children, here to pick him up. He let go of the thought of his mother, it was too hard to hold onto. He did not have the strength. Then it occurred to him how unusual it was to see his wife without the children. Since the twins were born his wife had changed. She was so taken up with them he hardly recognized her as the woman he had married.

A choice was before her. Either she could never move off the floor and stay forever among the folds of her green dress or get up quickly now and stand and do something. She thought, If I don't move now I never will and unthinking her hand reached for the bed and she pulled herself up. She was a little wobbly. She stepped and slipped on a little rag rug and the room lurched and the jolt shot her back into herself and her balance came instinctively back to her. She stood tingling in the middle of the room.

He had made his decision. Later in life Ann would learn that when certain men made decisions no matter how much it might torture them afterwards they would stick with their decision. Men, she learned, would rather suffer than change their minds or their habits. They could develop elaborate systems for containing pain, sometimes so successful they would remain completely unaware of the vastness of the pain they possessed.

She had to get out, she could not stay there.

But it was so tiring, one foot in front of the other. It was a long way back to the bed. She paused at the window and saw the edge of a stone bench and the white hydrangea Oscar liked glowing in the dusk and the shadows gathering beneath the bushes. *Oh god* a sharp pain in her side nearly split her in half *god that was a bad one.* She pressed all her weight onto the sill. The nausea passed and her vision cleared and she looked down to the dark ground and beneath her saw sprawled the coat he'd spread and the two of them lying on it. If every life had high points and low points there would have to be one point higher than the rest, the highest point in one's life. So, she learned, that had been hers.

A new thing had come to her after all.

A shadow moved beneath her. It was a person. She turned back toward the bed and saw a shadow under the door not moving. They were all around her, shadows moving and shadows not moving. No one knew who was watching whom.

She inched back to the bed and lay herself brittlely down. Across the ceiling his eyes appeared huge as parasols. Then he was sitting on the cedar chest at the foot of the bed, his shoulders and face turned away. She said his name. He dropped his chin in her direction showing that he heard her and tipped his ear toward her listening. Ann Lord did not get up again.

Lizzie Tull stepped over the raised threshold out of the throbbing room into the wind and the predawn light which was slashed by a yellow band along the horizon. She stood at the railing and dangled her hands in front of her with the water behind and stared past to the wake and waves without seeing any of it.

When the ferry docked in Rockland Harris Arden didn't wait for the ramp to lower before stepping on and hurrying over to Lizzie who came out of the violet shadows with her arms crossed, shaking her head. We lost him halfway over, she said.

Harris Arden opened the heavy black door of the passenger area for her as Vernon Tobin stepped out. Vernon had an unusual stare and after one step tipped forward with his feet rooted to the floor. Harris Arden caught him and eased him back inside.

It's O.K., he's just fainted, said Harris Arden, as he and Lizzie Tull slumped Vernon Tobin onto the nearest seat.

The Wittenborns and the doctor down at the other end of the passenger cabin beside the body on the cot all looked to see another body being carried in the door. They looked without surprise, watching the way animals register the approach of a human in the distance, waiting to measure the danger before deciding there's no need to run. Their faces looked as if they would never register surprise again.

Mrs. Wittenborn's arm was curved around the head of her son.

She took off her dress. The dress belonged to the night and to him and she would never wear it again. She stepped out of it and put on pants and a shirt and tennis shoes and left the room.

There were no people in sight when she came out of the cottage and walked up the wet grass. It was growing lighter and instead of feeling hope with the lifting of the darkness she felt the beginning of all the battles she would have to wage for the rest of her life. She followed the dark footprints up the hill and where they turned toward the house she left them and took the path down to the shore. She would see him again, but it would not be the same. She felt the tug of fatigue inside her but also felt strangely airy. They were all asleep by now she thought and she wondered if Harris was sleeping too or if he'd gone first to the other woman. She wondered if he'd kissed her yet.

But no one had been asleep.

Lila and Carl were awake at the inn getting ready to catch their plane. Later when they called from the airport in Boston to say good-bye they were unable to get through. The phones on Three O'Clock Island, all three numbers, were busy.

Lila would never forgive her mother for not letting them know, for keeping her from knowing what any stranger who picked up the Boston papers Monday morning knew when they read about the accident on page three or what anyone stepping up the soft steps of the general store on Three O'Clock Island would overhear about the Wittenborn wedding. Gigi tried to persuade her mother to call them, but Linda Wittenborn found this was one thing she could still control. She could at least allow her daughter to have the one honeymoon she would ever have. Lila never wanted to think of that honeymoon again.

She thought instead of what she'd missed—their house on Brattle Street full of people mourning Buddy and how she'd never know the long nights of sandwiches put out at midnight and the card games and the radio playing the ball game behind the discussion of funeral arrangements and drinks being made morning noon and night and the flowers coming in and the letters piling up. Lila could read the letters kept in the ribboned boxes but she never saw the coffin in the church aisle or watched it being lowered into the ground at Mt. Auburn Cemetery or heard Gigi reading Edward Thomas' "Rain" or seen Spring Tobin sprinkling dirt trance-like into the grave.

When Lila and Carl returned from their honeymoon they were met at the airport by all the Wittenborns standing there with terrible smiles. Lila knew right away something was wrong. Back at the Brattle Street house she went immediately up to Buddy's room and stood in it feeling she was at the top of a mountain in thin air. She felt she'd turned into a block of wood except for the flame of fury inside at her mother. Buddy's clothes were still folded in his drawers and his jackets were still hanging on their hangers. His shoes had the laces tied because he kicked off his shoes and she thought how his fingers had tied those knots. On his bedside table were some paperbacks, the top one was Raymond Chandler. A glass ashtray had a penny and some golf tees in it. Lila picked up a yellow tee and felt Buddy's tooth marks on the stem.


Margie and Constance were reading the cards.

Ralph and Kit Eastman. These are pretty. This gardenia's from Mr. Shepley.

That's nice.

Margie picked a small envelope off a plastic prong stuck into orange and yellow lilies. This is from . . . Geoffrey.

Who's that?

He does her hair.

Who's this? It came yesterday. Constance took a card out of the bowl. Maria Arden.

I don't know. I asked Mother but . . . Margie shrugged.

What'd she say?

She said No.


Ann Grant walked down to the shore sensing none of the tumult going on behind the trees back at the house. She was absorbed by her own tumult. Later when she compared the losses she judged herself selfish and wanted to disassociate herself from all that had mattered to her that night. The thought that she might have prevented Harris from helping was too much to face.

The tide had turned and was going out but the beach was still narrow with yellow and black seaweed flopped on the wet rocks. A long yellow cloud hovered at the horizon. Ann Grant left her clothes in a pile. She shivered though the air was mild, it would be another hot day. The water was smooth with a molten surface and she waded in, cutting off her thighs, and waded in further, cutting off her waist, then dove forward into the yellow sheen. With her eyes closed she saw Harris Arden's face and the way he'd been came back to her and she felt how changed she was after him and how she could never feel the same from now on and at least could take that with her. She thought of how much people changed you. It was the opposite of what you always heard, that no one could change a person. It wasn't true. It was only through other people that one ever did change.

The water was cold. She swam through it feeling strong in her legs and shoulders and it seemed that the strength came from him and as long as she felt that strength he would not leave her completely. Her changed self had his mark on it.

The trees on shore formed a dark wall tapering off to the left and tapering further into the distance on the other side. The sky grew brighter and she thought how the sky cared nothing for what happened beneath it and she tried to take some of that neutrality into herself. The water came up just under her nose and she swam and thought what had happened was hardly a universal tragedy. A dull pain sat in her as she thought this. Who ever said that one got what one wanted. It was a small thing compared to . . . well, to a lot of things. She'd gotten over things before *none like this* she'd left things behind *this was more* she couldn't speak of it *this was the first thing only hers* she would have to forget. *It was too great it was her heart.* She couldn't explain and to try and to fail would be worse. *It pressed in her.* Life simply went on. He was not the only man. *Her heart did not believe it.* There were other men in the world. *There was only one.* She would try to live a life he would be proud of. *She could not imagine it.* She would always have him with her. *He would go he would disappear he was already disappearing already he was gone.* He had given her a great thing. *He has gone, said her heart.* She would not let this defeat her. *Her heart swam on ahead.* She would keep going, she would never speak of it. *Her heart went on without her.* No one would know. She swam through the cold water and let cold reason take over and the heart which had asked for too much left her behind and when she emerged from the water on the rocky beach she had let go of it and there was a new version in her, a sort of second heart. She went in with one heart and came out with a second heart inside.

From her bed Ann Lord watched the figure swimming through the yellow dawn and saw herself for a moment as someone else might have seen her objectively and felt oddly compassionate and wondered at her thoughts. Had that really been herself? Then she saw a strange thing. A smooth mound of water rose glistening alongside the swimmer and Ann Lord felt it rising in her own chest, a little wave curling alongside staying with her, saying *I am here swimming up from this sea beside you I am here I have always been here your true self I was never gone and though you thought it came from him it was really yourself your whole self entire swimming underwater all the time there beside you I was always there beside your gliding boats and your flapping boats and your humming grinding boats all along I have been alongside you I have always been here I never left.*

In the morning Ann Lord asked to see a priest.

Nina's head popped in the door. Oh Mr. Granger, she said. Sorry, I didn't know anyone was in here.

Oliver Granger pointed to the bed. Sleeping, he mouthed.

Nina tiptoed in. She making any sense? she whispered.

She's making perfect sense. She says the apostles are calling.

As Nina gazed down at her mother, Oliver Granger stole a glance at her. Over the years he'd stolen many glimpses of Nina Lord wading at the Promontory picnic on the Fourth of July or sucking on a Popsicle at the Labor Day parade. He saw her in cut-offs and big shirts like the other girls and as she got older thrift shop dresses like ones his own mother used to wear but torn at the seams. He and Lily had seen her in *The Crucible* in western Massachusetts—Lily had family in the Berkshires—and Nina had starred in the Three O'Clock Island benefit production of *Carousel*. But Oliver Granger had hardly exchanged a word with Nina Lord.

Ann Lord's breath grew labored and they left the room together. Nina started down the stairs.

Mr. Granger, do you know a man named Harris? Some friend of Mother's.

There's Larry Harris from Newport. I'm not sure if your mother really knew . . .

We think it's his first name.

Harris . . . Harris . . .

Suddenly for no good reason Oliver Granger remembered the fellow at Carl and Lila's wedding that terrible weekend. He was that doctor . . . Arlen was his name, Harris Arlen. There now what would Lily say to that? Always accusing him of forgetting every-thing, here was something he didn't forget. Oliver had seen him again, Harris Arlen, by chance in Chicago . . . was it Arlen? something like that anyway . . . must have been ten years after he'd driven him that morning to the Wittenborns' boat, he didn't forget that either . . . he'd seen him outside the museum in Chicago waiting for Lily to buy her postcards . . . Harris Arlen was with a beautiful woman wearing a man's suit and no makeup, a woman clearly not his wife, quite remarkable-looking . . . Oliver remembered the woman almost more than he'd remembered Harris Arlen.

Your Uncle Carl had a friend named Harris, said Oliver. Rather dashing figure.

Nina stopped on the stairs. Who was he?

A doctor from Chicago. He came to their wedding. Played a frightful saxophone I remember.

Dashing?

Rather a ladies' man.

Nina looked thoughtful. She's been saying his name.

Oliver looked over Nina's head. You know your mother might be thinking of him—Oliver congratulated himself on making the subtle connection—because he was a doctor. He tried to save someone's life. Your mother must have told you what happened at the Cutlers' wedding.

Sort of, Nina said. But what was it again.

She sat on the step below and Oliver Granger told her the story everyone knew, not mentioning anything about a rock garden or a sail closet or the ground by the Lorings' dock, not knowing any of that, having Nina Lord's attention for longer than he'd had it all told in their lifetimes, ending his account with his putting Harris Arlen on the *Happenstance*, a boat known to Nina Lord—she'd kissed Lila's son Buddy Cutler in it when she was thirteen—but not adding that after the boat had motored off Gail Slater had collapsed in his arms in tears. That was a detail he had forgotten.

Nina listened with a beady stare. So where was Harris?

Oliver Granger thought a moment. He had a fiancée there, I suppose with her. No . . . it was . . . you know, I can't remember.

Nina looked penetratingly at Mr. Granger. Could he have saved Buddy Wittenborn?

Oliver Granger slapped his thighs and stood up. Something we'll never know, he said.


When she came up from the shore she saw lights on in the big house and in the driveway Ollie Granger's car back again and thought they'd certainly had a long night without her. She looked down to the end of the house to the room Harris Arden was sharing with Ralph Eastman. Its window was dark.

A car was coming toward her down the driveway. Ann Grant was surprised to see Mr. and Mrs. Tobin. It couldn't have been much after six o'clock, a little early for breakfast. She had spoken very little to Vernon's parents over the weekend and they were the last people she would've chosen to run into. It occurred to her they might have been up to see Lila and Carl off at the inn. The car slowed down and Mr. Tobin rolled down his window.

Are they back yet? He was frowning and his usually jaunty voice was flat.

No, she said, thinking he meant Lila and Carl. They weren't coming back.

They weren't? Mr. Tobin looked with alarm at his wife.

Mrs. Tobin leaned forward to see Ann's face. They're going straight down to Boston then? She had an odd expression.

I think so, yes.

Mrs. Tobin sat back. They must be bringing him down, she muttered, and clutched Mr. Tobin's arm. Ann thought their behavior most strange.

Mr. Tobin glanced toward the house. Who's up? he said.

Ann said she didn't know.

What? Mrs. Tobin's face was hard. She'd never liked Ann.

I was swimming, Ann said.

The Tobins looked at her with disbelief. Mrs. Tobin said, Were you there?

Suddenly Ann Grant realized something else was going on and that that something else was terribly wrong. Where? she said.

The Tobins exchanged glances.

Then Mrs. Tobin told her what happened and as Ann listened the surreal feeling of the night increased. It flipped into another world. Ann noticed with horror that Mrs. Tobin seemed excited to tell it.

Though it was clear she had not known, the Tobins never forgot their first impression of running into Ann Grant that morning and of how oddly she'd behaved, confirming what Mrs. Tobin had always thought, that Ann Grant was a cold girl.


They were milling around in a sort of basement, waiting for the music to begin. Everyone was there, Ted glancing indifferently over his shoulder, Oscar straightening the brim of his white hat. Paul had been crying and was trying to hide it then he disappeared in the crowd. They began to form a conga line. Everyone started to dance. She saw Kingie go by with a bandage taped to her throat and Buddy Wittenborn with his face unchanged but his body aged and his waist thick. They followed one another, throwing out a leg, holding onto the hips in front of them. Dick and Linda Wittenborn were all in white and Ann's mother wore an orange dress which she never would have chosen with a Balinese headdress and her mouth twisted to the side. Her father was wearing purple lipstick. She saw Don Shepley's brother in a lamb's-wool hat and Phil thin as a rail with brown teeth. Mrs. Futter from Gray Gable Road was in her apron, but it was upside-down and Mr. Tobin had no arms. Aunt Joy's hair was red and fluffy and Elsie Roland's father whom she'd met once handed her an electric baton. Abbott was in her uniform with the blue velvet hat she wore to church and wearing her hospital gown was the bald woman named Gwenivere who'd been in the hospital room beside her. They all cha-chaed by.

# FIVE

*The line is a churning twister . . . Stand up, Stand up . . . alone!*

# 16. EVENING

*G*od *why won't it stop it has been barking all night*

It was dawn and her room was suddenly full of people sitting at tables smoking cigarettes wearing tweeds and giving orders for breakfast.

Her throat was dry, no air was going down. Help me, she thought, help me. She tried to speak but could only wheeze. Something was making the bed vibrate then it turned close, and became her moaning. *Help me.* Pillows were propped against the headboard and on either side of her was a row of people wired up to one another like a telephone switchboard. They passed along a small white cup. When the cup reached her she was careful not to spill it, the goal being to move your body as little as possible.

Then it was all wrong and she was sleeping in screens, the sheets had turned into screens. The mesh was raw on her skin. The ceiling was frowning. It said no one knows what life is for, no one knows what anything means, the plaster soft and uneven, the lines as thin as the cracks in one's palm, it said silence wipes everything out.


They didn't bring Buddy back. Mrs. Wittenborn wanted to stay with the body—it was being flown back to Boston—but her husband wouldn't allow it. You ought to stay with Gigi, he said, and when Gigi offered to stay he said, no your mother needs you. Whereas it was he who needed the two of them, too frightened to be alone. He had loved his son from his distant column and did not dare think how it felt to lose him and having women weeping around him made him think he was feeling this thing he dared not approach with feeling. He was a man who had married a younger woman because she was so far from what he was and the thing he most wished was to be not bothered.

When the Wittenborns came back and Ann saw their faces what had happened became real. The air in the house overlooking the bay was full of phones ringing and visitors and tossed-off loose laughter and tears and a sense not proud but automatic of importance. People stood close to one another, they lay on the floor. They ate sandwiches as they walked across the lawn. They told the story of the night before again and again, and Ann Grant listened again and again to all the versions and there were small new things each time but no new meaning.

More stories came later. Foy Hopkin's sister Audrey had been driving to work in town where she ran the shortwave radio for the lobster boats when she saw a figure walking near the turn-off to the Promontory. Finding it unusual to see emerging from the morning haze a young man in a dress suit she stopped and asked him if he wanted a ride. He came to the window and she saw it was Buddy Wittenborn. She knew Buddy Wittenborn, she used to baby-sit for him. She asked him how the wedding was—everyone on the island knew about the Wittenborn wedding, her niece had served at the reception and Foy's brother-in-law had dug the clams they ate at the Yacht Club—and Buddy said it had been a pretty good wedding. He said he felt like walking but thanks anyway for the ride. Everyone said it must have been Ralph Eastman but no one could explain the detail Audrey had mentioned on the radio to the Julep brothers before she'd heard about the accident, that she'd seen Buddy Wittenborn that morning, and it must have been a wild wedding because the glasses he had on his face were broken in two.

And he came back too, Harris came back. He was there among the people hurrying down halls and carrying suitcases and moving cars in the driveway. The woman Maria sat patiently at the end of the veranda holding a cup of tea and saucer, pale and composed, looking up when Harris went past with a gaze for only him.

Ann was coming out of the pantry with a can of coffee and Eve Wittenborn went by carrying a platter of deviled ham sandwiches into the dining room as Harris came in. For a moment he and she were alone in the kitchen. They were changed from how they'd been a few hours before. They did not speak of themselves, they did not speak. Ann could feel Harris looking at her as she opened the tin of coffee. Finally she said, I keep expecting him to walk in the door, and they looked at one another and Ann thought she saw a glint of fear in his eye. Then Lizzie Tull burst in looking for napkins and Mrs. Slater entered from the back door with a pitcher of Bloody Marys which she said she thought everyone could use and Ann realized that that must have been the last thing she'd ever said to Harris Arden. *I keep expecting him to walk in the door.*

There was no other good-bye though she did see him leave. Upstairs in Gigi's room helping her pack Ann heard another car start and looked down to the driveway and saw the top of a hatbox next to Maria's head. Harris followed carrying bags. Mrs. Tobin was sitting in the front seat. Mr. Tobin and Harris loaded the trunk then snapped it down. Ralph Eastman came out from under the porch and shook Harris' hand and Harris embraced him. Ann saw Harris wave to someone under the porch roof out of sight. Maria ducked into the car then Harris got in, his shoulders crowding the space. She saw his legs in light-colored pants facing forward. He pulled shut the door. The glass on the car window was a maze of reflections of light and shadows and leaves and sky, moving when the car drove away, and the reflection blocked her from seeing the person inside.

Later she stood on the lawn among the last to leave.

Ann, she heard. His voice went through her, low, shaking her, and she turned around and he wasn't there. She opened her eyes and he wasn't there.

Ann, she thought. Let her go.

And she began to let go, she let go of the soaked grass and the humped hills and the headlights sweeping the driveway and the steep night with the band's dwindling notes, she released his collar and his sleeve and his hand and dropped the jangling latch of the screen door, she lifted her palm from the oilcloth on the table and let go of the stars which had been too bright and the pale black sky and dropped like a stone the sight of him leaving through the window not having said good-bye, she let go of the flagpole with its sulky flap and left behind the path cut through the tall grass and the steps with the moss and the rocks uneven under her feet and the cold water lapping at her throat. She let go of all of it.

It had left her once and after all this time had come back and the only thing to prevent its coming again was her not being there to receive it and that was something which would happen of its own accord. That was not something she needed to control.

She saw her sunglasses in the train window.

She could see her father's shadowed head against the colored bottles at the bar. *Here's my angel of mercy come to fetch me.*

She had been on the train for a long time, for days, there were veils covering her face, outlining her profile, and each time she passed into a different state the wind took one off blowing it out the narrow slot of the train window, a bleached potato sack flying into the wet green gorge of Pennsylvania after a storm with thun-

der receding, a linen runner into the violet mist of the hills above
Nashville, brown taffeta blew out over the flattened yellow fields
where the Mississippi River had withdrawn and white farmhouses
sat like sugar cubes in the distance, out went the ivory lace into a
pink sky over lumped trees, a gingham kerchief into the beige dust
blown up as the train whizzed by the candy cane railroad signals
clanging, dry husks filled her mouth and partridges flushed out of
the shaking grass, out flew a cotton towel nearly transparent from
use as she clattered past lots on the outskirts of towns clogged with
skunk cabbage and mustard weed with scraps of newspaper snowing down and plastic bags plastered to chain link fences, rust shav-
ings glinting in heaps near Chicago and guardhouse panes rattling
in their frames, a veil thin as mosquito net was whisked over the
flooded cranberry bogs and twisted Wisconsin trees, over the lakes
in Minnesota, mirrors reflecting nothing, all were sucked out the
window flying off her dozing face, the veils which had been put on
all her life coming off now one at a time till she got to the final
black one which would not come off.


*Let's see our temperature* her brain was boiling, she was supposed
to choose between a kitchen and an ocean *stop crying she can hear
you* what did they want? She wanted to be left alone but didn't
want them to go away, she didn't want anyone to go away, a milk
bottle with a red pleated top, they didn't realize what was going on
*I'll be back tomorrow Ann* they were always going, they always
went, they didn't ever stay.

She asked them why but they wouldn't tell her.

*See you soon* today was Friday tomorrow was Tuesday then it
was Friday again *I don't think she can hear you very well* what? a
pill pushing her lips *take this then* it muddled her mind she only
had her mind left *I don't think she recognizes me* I don't think

They sat on a terrace with small coffee cups, he came out from
behind a tree in the hot wind after rain a shutter was banging
*leave the table alone and come here* the windows had been sited

just right for the sunset, the kitchen should have been on the north side. When they moved in the downstairs was a ghastly green, she repainted right away, Abbott kept the linens neat. She redid the library, the sofa was reupholstered with the zippers inside out, the floor needed a rug, which room was she in? *I'm right here.* The cabinet latches were too high *would anyone like another drink?* She had to get rid of all that junk *I better go* one room kept turning into a closet *I better go* they should have left on the front light *where have you been?* the gardener cut down the lilac bush by mistake, she planted daffodils in clusters, the vases needed to be changed *don't forget* before closing the house the curtains should be draped over sawhorses *don't forget* paper put between the sheets, the fireplace ashes saved *easy to put together, hard to take apart* she couldn't remember which house it was *who would like some more?* there was forsythia on the hall table in the spring, her mother kept the mail in a pile, her father leaned on the railing coming down the steps, she was dancing with him on flagstones his skin began to leak *where's Nora?* There was nothing she could do about the stairs, they couldn't be changed, she would have to live with them *where are you?* She heard them going by out in the hall whispering *back tomorrow!* The highboy cracked down the center *Nora* She opened the door to the hall in the middle of the night and was stopped by a sheer rock face *what is she saying? She wants the nurse* waves were washing down the stairs *we'll be back tomorrow Ann* the twins in corduroy jackets matching *when are you coming back?* their shoulder blades like birds *back tomorrow see you*

Down in the cellar they were slicing white pineapple and slabs of white whale meat *Nora where's Nora?* They were cutting white flesh *where was her heart?* She used to have a madonna in gold leaf by her bed *she said she'd never leave me* she used to have a white halter dress she used to sing in the choir she trimmed the girls' hair she had a rose garden *Nora*

*I'm right here*

This was not just a day trip, her parents were going on a pilgrimage

*We'll say a prayer for you* the smell of rose water, you dipped your finger in and made the sign of the cross *I better go they said I better go* ribbons marked the place in the rice pages *have you forgotten? I'm right here don't forget* think of those less fortunate *don't forget, that's nonsense, don't forget, stop being absurd*

*Let's turn you over*

*The thing is it only hurts when it hurts* she said her prie-dieus *I better go* her mother taught her to make stew *first brown the meat* they had cake at tea she took a sunbath *don't be absurd* they celebrated D-Day by taking a swim *don't be ridiculous* she bought a red winter coat an evening dress from Bonwit Teller she tried on a darling bathing suit but they had no charge at Neal's *but the thing is it hurts all the time* they went starlight coasting she had lunch with Lila at Schraffts' he brought her a gardenia they talked about two things what they did was a secret *that's nonsense* Frank was in the parlor shaking change in his pocket it had snowed the steps were deep and white after the party they went to bed at six they hit a snowbank on the way home and had to crawl in the window his cheek was hot he lifted her *the way you looked made me want to kiss you* her mouth turned into a sea anemone a hand was clamped over her mouth *one day there will be no dawn* they went to a double feature she forgot her wallet and scarf they walked home *I don't have any news* the tar was warm through her tennis shoes the trees were black *that's alright you don't have to say anything* she might have had another life *don't be absurd* another woman had her life he carried it off in his pocket *it endures inside he said* she was a tray of bones she was pregnant again *where is inside? can we go there together?* other people were living in her apartment a cyclone was coming her father went up to the church balcony without warning anyone about the storm *it is all in the mind* the baby was wrapped in a blanket then it began to unravel in the wind till all that was left was a little wooden stick *there are no oceans in the mind* she was the same age as her mother *first there is the world then the mind comes after* her soul was turning down *so being there first is important after all* there was no more *stay like that always* she was so small *she says she'll never leave me* no more to say or do or think or be *don't be that way that's nonsense* he once touched her lips *then what are you doing* that was *don't stop* that was *don't leave* that was all *don't forget don't be absurd don't be* that was *stay like that always* don't forget me *don't be absurd I won't* don't forget me *I will always I will never I will always*

August 3 11-7

11am Juice 1 tsp No reaction when spoken to Respiration labored 16 R/98.6 Unable to count pulse Very weak   11:45 Perspiring Gown changed Sponge bath Care to hips and back Pos changed   12:15 Called me by name Juice one sip   1:15 Morphine sulfate ½ cc as ordered Juice 1 tsp Moaning   2:00 Juice sip (spoon) Pos changed Back and hips rubbed   3:45 Juice sip Pos changed Care to hips and back 4:15 Morphine sulphate as ordered   5:15 Juice sip   6:00 Sponge bath Care to hips and back Hair combed Pos changed R/98.6 Resp 16 labored Pulse weak Has not voided Intake nil

It could happen anytime. It could happen tonight.
Yes well we thought that Thursday.
You can't tell. Nora said you can't predict.
Was Dr. Baker here this morning?
Around noon he came.
What did he say?
That it could be anytime.
Very helpful.
Would it make a difference if we knew? I mean really.
We could . . . I don't know . . . plan. We could . . . we'd just know.
It wouldn't make a difference. We'd still be waiting. That's all we can do. Be here and wait.
I wouldn't *want* to know myself, Nina said.
I wonder if she's finished up there, Teddy said.
We can wait another minute.
Is that the fountain on out there?
No.
Yes it is. Listen.

Who turned it on?

They all looked at each other. No one spoke.

God, Constance said.

It's a nice sound, Margie said.

They listened to the water running in the dark.

August 4 7-3

7am Patient in same weakened state a.m. care turned and position changed Bed changed R/99.6 Pulse very weak Resp 16 labored   8:00 Patient moaning Appears very uncomfortable Morphine sulfate 15 mg IM Skin clammy to touch   8:15 Dr Baker in Condition remains same Void of intake   9:00 Son T.S. phoned Turned and positioned Skin care oral care X2 0 pulse Resp 14-16 labored breathing Unresponsive 10:00 Moaning unconsciously Both pupils constricted Backward arching of neck and shoulders noted Legs appear rigid Oral care 11:00 Position changed Turned Skin care oral care Moaning   12 Noon Turned 0 void Still moaning Morphine sulfate 15 mg IM for pain Congestion noted 0 pulse Resp very labored   1 pm Turned over Resp 10-12 1:10 0 response 0 pulse Body convulsions Vomitus expelled from oral cavity Dr Baker notified Daughters present Son present in room 1:30 Dr. Baker in to verify expiration.

N. Brown, LPN

❉   ❉   ❉

I'm going to have to go.

Yes, I know.

Her mouth was parted and her breath rattled in her throat. After a silence she said, Will you come back.

Of course!

Tomorrow? You'll come back tomorrow?

I'll do my best. But it may have to be the day after.

He waited a moment or two then said very softly, Are you asleep? Little angel?

No, I'm not asleep.

I will try to come tomorrow. But it's complicated. It's been lovely to see you, he said.

Yes, she said. So lovely. My father used to call me angel, she murmured.

I won't say good-bye.

No, she said. Don't.

He did not come the next day, he did not come the day after. He did not come again.

Susan Minot was born in Boston, Massachusetts, and grew up in Manchester-by-the-Sea. Her first novel, *Monkeys*, was published in a dozen countries and received the Prix Femina Étranger in France. She is the author of *Lust & Other Stories* and *Folly*, a novel, and wrote the screenplay for Bernardo Bertolucci's *Stealing Beauty*.

A NOTE ON THE TYPE

This book was set in Caledonia, a typeface designed by W. A. Dwiggins (1880–1956). It belongs to the family of printing types called "modern face" by printers—a term used to mark the change in style of type letters that occurred about 1800. Caledonia borders on the general design of Scotch Roman, but is more freely drawn than that letter.

Composed by North Market Street Graphics,
Lancaster, Pennsylvania
Printed and bound by The Haddon Craftsmen,
Bloomsburg, Pennsylvania
Typography and binding design by Dorothy S. Baker